Praise for ?

"A thrilling mystery wrapped in a compelling coming-of-age story set in early twentieth-century Brewster, New York. I couldn't get enough of the spot-on period details of my hometown. Deborah Oswald has a knack for describing the beauties of upstate New York."

—Gail Carson Levine, author of *Ella Enchanted*

To Michelle,
A dear friend and
a lover of literature

Love,
Debbi

Visit Deborah at www.deborahraffertyoswald.com

Also by Deborah Rafferty Oswald

The Girls of Haviland

Beyond Haviland

by
Deborah Rafferty Oswald

Print Edition
ISBN: 978-1-730-87594-6

Cover illustration by Lisa Fields

For Chuck, Caragh, Annie, and Katie

Chapter One

"Who are all these people? I don't recognize any-one." I strained my neck in the pouring rain to see around the Model T in front of us. "We've been stuck in this line for over an hour, and I'm late for check-in."

"Traffic's stopped dead for as far as I can see with the fog coming in off the lake." Henry jumped down from the rig. "Mulligan's getting restless, and Maisie looks like a wet mop." The horses snorted and stomped their hooves in the puddles on the rutted road. "This weather's no good for their joints."

"Oh, for heaven's sake. Don't look, Henry." I watched two girls jump out of a touring car and hold a blanket in front of an older woman who proceeded to relieve herself on the shore of Lake Gleneida. I wanted to die of embarrassment as my boyfriend witnessed this spectacle.

Henry busted out laughing. "Classy bunch, these Haviland folks."

I climbed down from the rig, the wind and rain slapping my face. "I can't wait any more. I'll just grab my things and walk the rest of the way. Your mother will never forgive me if I make you late for church."

"You can't carry everything all the way up to the dorm. Your trunk weighs a ton." Henry pulled my soaking laundry bag down from the back of the rig.

I gave him a wet hug and a quick kiss. "I'll manage. I'll write once I'm settled."

"Sure you will." Henry smirked before turning the rig around.

My arms felt about ready to fall off by the time I lugged my trunk up to the dorm, where I had to wait in line to sign in at the reception desk. The dark vestibule stunk of wet wool and too many bodies crammed together. My braid dripped water down my back. I dropped my book satchel when it was finally my turn and flexed my fingers, which had turned white from lack of blood circulation.

"What's going on here?" I wished Lydia, the former RA, was still here.

"It's been like this all morning." Betty Cornish pushed her glasses up the bridge of her nose and tucked a strand of frizzy hair behind one ear. "I don't know where they've all come from, and I'm the only RA on duty."

I grabbed the pen from her hand and dipped it in the inkwell. "Well, I know where I'm going, so I'll just sign in and leave you to deal with everyone else." I proceeded down the hall to Florence's room, my trunk thumping behind me.

"Jay, wait!" Betty came from behind the reception desk, leaving a chorus of complaints from the line of bedraggled parents and students.

I swung open the door of our room. "I'm back."

"Late as usual." Evangeline Sprague, my obnoxious roommate from sophomore year, was lying on my bed.

"What are you doing here? You left."

"Mother and I agreed that Miss Theriault's Academy was lacking, so I decided to resume my studies here," she explained. "Sans Mary Agnes, of course."

I cringed as I recalled the day that Evangeline's sister, Mary Agnes, revealed to me that she drove Violet Dean to commit suicide. Mercifully, she was expelled from Haviland.

Betty's flushed face looked about ready to explode. "I tried to catch you, Jay, to let you know there has been a huge increase in students this year, and it's resulted in a severe housing shortage."

"So what?" I said, pushing my trunk alongside Evangeline's. "Florence and I reserved this room before we left in June."

"Jay, let me explain," said Betty. "The new school administration has adopted a first come, first served policy to try to accommodate everyone. Evangeline was here at six o'clock this morning and therefore had her pick of rooms. She chose this one."

"So I'm stuck with the third bed?" I groaned.

Betty scanned her clipboard. "I'm sorry, Jay. That bed was claimed by Helen Starr at seven thirty this morning."

"Helen Starr? Where am I supposed to sleep, on the floor?"

"The early bird gets the worm, Jay." Evangeline plumped the pillow beneath her greasy head. I forced myself not to grab the pillow and hold it over her face.

Betty tapped the clipboard with her pen, spraying Pacific Blue ink all over my face. "Patience Hall is now completely filled. That's what I've been trying to tell you. You'll have to stay at the Fowler House. The Fowler sisters have agreed to board some of the overflow of students who have not been able to secure rooms."

"You mean I can't live in the dorm?" My lip started to tremble.

"Now, Jay, calm down." Betty brought my laundry bag into the hall. "The Fowler House is located on the entranceway to Haviland. I've been assured that you'll find their accommodations quite satisfactory. It's just a short walk. I'm confident you will be warmly welcomed." She glanced wearily at the growing line of disgruntled students and parents at the reception desk. "If you'll excuse me, I have to inform that whole line of families that their daughters must commute to school."

"Jay!" Florence was running down the thickly carpeted hall.

I caught up with her. "Evangeline took my bed."

"Where have you been?" Florence stopped to catch her breath.

My best friend was a sight for sore eyes, her sea-green eyes complementing her coffee-with-cream complexion.

Florence continued once she regulated her breathing. "I went to Dr. Wisdom to complain, but she's gone. There's a new headmistress, who told me the increase has something to do with the war being over. Haviland's never had this many new students, and there's no place to put them. I hear they're even admitting boys this year."

"I can't stay in the dorm, Florence!" I felt weary and wanted to go home. No I didn't. I wanted my room back.

Florence shut the door to the room so Evangeline couldn't snoop on our conversation. "Why are you so late? Evangeline didn't even want to let me into my own room. I had to get Betty to come down and insist that a third bed be moved in for you, Jay, but then Helen showed up at seven thirty, furious that she got kicked out of the room she shared with Nathalia last year. Mercy got here before her and claimed that bed. Now we're stuck with her."

"You mean *you're* stuck with her. And it's not my fault I'm late." I pointed to the school's entranceway still clogged with cars and wagons. "Traffic is backed up all the way down Gleneida Avenue."

"Well, we all managed to get here on time. Now I'm stuck with those two snobs. Thanks, a lot."

"I'm sorry, Florence. I had no idea. Listen, I've got to get out of these wet clothes, so I'd better get going." Dejected, I picked up my sodden bags.

"Don't go around with the puss on your face feeling sorry for yourself. Wait here while I grab my rain slicker. I'll drag this trunk down there for you."

We sloshed our way through the mud leading to the Fowler House. Carcasses of deer, rabbits, raccoons, and turkey vultures swung from tree branches, dripping blood-tinged water in the mud. Hills Brothers coffee cans, riddled with bullet holes, topped every fence post and tree stump.

"This isn't going to work." I grabbed the knocker and rapped it against the front door a few times. I realized too late that the door was left slightly ajar. At my knocking, six mangy dogs bolted through the door and charged us.

"Run!" I yelled. Teeth bared, the dogs jumped at us until we were corralled, trying to fight them off.

A tall, skinny old lady wearing a coonskin cap opened the door. She placed two fingers in her mouth and gave a shrill whistle. The dogs backed off, just a bit, still growling. Foamy drool dripped from their exposed gums.

"There's two more, Hazel," she called. "It's a sin having students move in on our Lord's day of rest. A sin against God, and I'll not have it."

5

"At least let them in out of the weather, Tillie." A short, stout lady descended the few rickety stairs leading from the house. She approached us, lifting her skirt up to her knees and holding a huge umbrella over her head.

"Call off your dogs," yelled Florence, above the barking. Her fingers dug into my upper arms.

"My apologies, ladies." The short lady shooed the wet mongrels up toward the house. "They're watchdogs, and not used to so many visitors." She summoned us in with her free hand. "I'm Miss Hazel Fowler, and that's my sister, Miss Tillie, at the door. Come inside."

From behind, the sisters resembled a hot dog and a hamburger.

The stink of cat pee hit me the moment I set foot through the door. I counted eight felines snoozing on the headrests of the sofa and Queen Anne chairs set before the fireplace. Cats tiptoed in and out through the rows of galoshes lined up inside the entryway. An orange tabby slinking around my ankles was wearing a knit bonnet tied under its chin.

I nudged Florence in her ribs and pointed to the fireplace. Mounted above the hearth was an enormous moose head, its face turned toward us. Its dark lips were set in a ghoulish grin. All four walls were covered with deer mounts, stuffed raccoons, pheasants, hawks, and what I thought might be a bobcat. One of its paws was raised, claws outstretched, ready to pounce.

"Look at its eyes," Florence whispered out of the side of her mouth. "I think it's watching us."

Several needlework Bible verses were displayed among the dead animals. One read: "If anyone curses his father or mother, he must be put to death. Leviticus 20:9."

I wondered how many times I had cursed Da when he was alive.

"Here, let me take those wet things for you, ladies." Miss Hazel assisted us out of our soaking school blazers and hats. "Sit by the fire and dry off while I pour tea."

I checked for cat droppings before tentatively taking a seat.

Miss Tillie, dressed in black mourning, was seated in a rocking chair close to the stingy light of the window. Without looking up from her Bible, she said, "Afraid you ladies made a trip for nothing in this weather. At last count, there were ten students settling in upstairs."

"Well, then, we won't be wasting any more of your time." I rose up from the chair upon which I had never fully sat down.

"Nonsense, sister." Miss Hazel placed a silver tea set down on the table. "We can make do."

Florence scrutinized her cup of tea before taking a sip. "I'm staying up at Patience Hall. It's only Jay here that needs a bed."

Hazel clapped her plump hands. "You see, Tillie? I was just saying that there was only one bed available." She turned her attention back to her sister. "So it's all settled then."

Miss Tillie snorted in disgust. She was silhouetted by ten drippy candles burning on the windowsills and side table.

"Do you require assistance with your luggage?" asked Miss Hazel. "We have a young man boarding with us, on the first floor of course, must think of propriety. He's been helping the ladies with their trunks all morning. I'll call him." She cupped her hand at the side of her tiny mouth. "Yoo hoo, Will!"

"He's not one of your cats, sister," snarled Tillie.

"That won't be necessary." I stared at the kitten lapping

up tea from the saucer I had put down on the coffee table. "I'm not even sure I'll be staying."

"Suit yourself." Miss Hazel led us up a narrow staircase. As we ascended each stair, the cat pee stench mingled with the smell of talcum powder and body odor.

"Well, here we are." She spread her chubby arms wide as we reached the second floor. "We're a little cramped, but I think we can manage."

"For Pete's sake, not another one," said one of the girls, smoothing an eiderdown quilt across a narrow bed.

My stomach dropped as I surveyed the scene in front of me. A double row of dingy cots and iron-framed beds lined a drafty attic with loose floorboards and a few cracked windows. Rain dripped from the ceiling, collecting in laundry tubs placed strategically throughout the cramped space. Wet underwear hung from a clothesline that crisscrossed overhead on the boards below the vaulted ceiling.

"You honestly can't expect her to stay here," said Florence, a vein throbbing in the space between her eyebrows.

"I know it looks rather dreary up here in the rain, but I assure you it will brighten up quite a bit in the sunshine," said Miss Hazel. "Come with me."

We negotiated our way through the maze of staring girls, beds, and trunks.

"See the line of maples along the entranceway to the school?" Miss Hazel pointed out a window fogged with condensation. A crack in her fingernail was filled with dirt. "In a few weeks they will be ablaze with fiery color, and this is the best view on the property."

"I'm not leaving you here," Florence said. "You're bound to catch some rare cat disease." She shooed an enormous gray calico away. "Scat! Go away!"

The cat hissed and leapt up at Florence, scratching her knuckles.

"You little beast!" She brought her hand up to inspect the wound.

"You mustn't mind Felicity," Miss Hazel said, scooping up the bloated cat. "She gets rather territorial whenever she's about to birth a new litter." She looked Florence up and down. "She doesn't take kindly to...strangers."

"Do the cats think I'm getting too uppity?" Florence challenged her. "For a colored girl, that is?"

Miss Hazel's eyes widened in mortification. She jumped back on her feet, which seemed too tiny to support her ample girth. "I certainly meant no offense."

"You don't have to do this, Jay," said Florence. "I can smuggle you into our dorm room somehow, after dark, maybe."

"With Evangeline there? She'd give me up in a heart-beat." I looked around. "I've no choice. I'll put my name on a waiting list for a dorm room and stay here for now."

"So you'll be joining us?" Miss Hazel asked.

"We both will," said Florence.

"What are you talking about?" I asked. "You have a nice bed in Patience Hall waiting for you. Go on, get going. I'll be fine."

"You'll never survive here without me," said Florence. "And I'm demanding a substantial discount on your room and board bill as well as mine. I paid for you to stay in Patience Hall, not this dump."

I grinned, realizing Florence preferred this leaky attic to the dorm room with Evangeline and Helen. When I lost my Borden's scholarship last spring, Florence had paid for my room and board with some of the money she inher-ited from her late father's estate. Still, I couldn't let her do this, although I loved her for offering. "You're talking crazy, and plus, there's barely enough room for me."

"Miss Hazel, I can grab my quilt and blankets from the dorm and make a bed right here across from Jay. That is, unless you have a policy against boarding colored girls."

"Uh, no, I mean, that will be fine," sputtered Miss Hazel. "There's some space down there near the end, I believe." Miss Hazel started toward the far side of the room. She rummaged through a stack of dusty paintings leaning against the wall. "Aha! Brother's old army cot. And here is dear Father's sickbed mattress. I knew they were behind here somewhere." She dragged out the filthy cot first, summoning Florence and me to haul out the stained mattress with rusted springs poking up through tears in the fabric. "Will can assemble these in a jiffy here against the wall."

"There's no way you'll be able to fit in there," I said.

"Why, there's plenty of room," said Miss Hazel. "Plus, you get the added advantage of being close to the storage closet." She beamed as she motioned toward an open trap door exposing a space crammed with rusted paint cans, hat boxes, and stacks of newspapers.

I looked around to see which window I could jump out of when this place caught fire, which I was positive would be very soon.

"Well, what do you say, ladies?"

"Florence, don't do this." I tried to shake loose a black kitten that'd dug its claws into my sweater. This was a bad omen, for sure.

"I'm not leaving you alone here. You're going to help me fetch my things from the dorm. End of story."

Within an hour, we dragged our trunks between the double rows of beds, ducking under the dripping laundry.

"How're you all faring on this fine Sunday?" asked Florence, smiling at the glaring faces of the rows of girls. One girl gave us a smile though. I hoped she wasn't crazy. The crazy ones always tried to be your friend first.

I groaned at the black mold growing along the seams of the assembled army cot. "How am I ever going to sleep on this?" It sagged low to the ground and seemed barely sturdy enough to support my weight.

"You're kidding me, right?" Florence was layering folded blankets on her filthy mattress to cushion the exposed springs.

Setting my trunk at the foot of the bed, I dug through my belongings until I reached my bed sheets, miraculously still dry.

The girl who smiled at us stood two beds over from mine. She was singing a song in a foreign language, revealing perfect white teeth. Her glossy, black hair was done in Mary Pickford curls, which somehow survived this rainy morning. There must have been twenty ringlets hanging halfway down her back.

A plop of water landed on her head, and she scooted over to move a steel washtub under the new leak. She smiled again. "Welcome to The Plaza Hotel."

"More like the Haviland flophouse," I said.

The girl pointed to the bed between us and put her finger to her lips. "Shh, you'll wake Sleeping Beauty."

Sure enough, there was a mound under a crocheted throw in the bed next to me. I watched the rise and fall of her breathing under the blanket. Who could sleep in such chaos?

"That one's been out cold since I got here this morning," the girl with the ringlets continued. "Miss Hazel said she showed up at the crack of dawn with nothing but a dirty old sack." The girl had long-lashed eyes as black as her hair. She spoke with an accent. Spanish, I guessed.

"You're new here, right?" I asked, certain I'd never seen her before.

She nodded. "Maria del Pilar Hoyas y Bailey, from Key West, Florida."

"Wow, that's a mouthful. I'm Josephine Bernadette Margaret McKenna, but everybody calls me Jay. This is my friend, Florence."

"Everybody calls me Pilar. I was just showing off." When she started laughing, I knew I'd found a kindred spirit.

A girl on the other end of the attic lit a cigarette and passed it down the line of girls.

Pilar scrunched up her nose. "Yuck. Get that thing away from me."

"What, you've never sneaked a cigarette before?" the offended owner teased.

"I smoke only the finest Cuban cigars." Pilar held her hand up to silence the girls. "Put that thing out. I hear someone coming."

Sure enough, heavy footsteps sounded on the stairs. I made a mental note to ask Pilar about the cigars some other time.

"Ladies, now that you've unpacked, Miss Tillie and I request that you join us in the parlor for tea and conversation." Miss Hazel carefully made her way back downstairs.

"Hey, wake up." I gave a little shake to whoever was sleeping next to my cot. "We have to go downstairs."

The mound growled, "Go away."

"Leave that nasty old thing to fend for herself," said Florence.

*

Within minutes, the lot of us filed downstairs and made our way into the musty, cramped parlor.

"There's a squirrel on top of that birdcage!" Florence grabbed a corn broom leaning against the front door to shoo it outside.

Miss Hazel chuckled and summoned the rodent, who hopped off the cage onto her shoulder. "This is Baxter, ladies. We're old friends, and he's completely house-broken. I couldn't imagine life without him."

"She's nuts to have a squirrel in the house," I said. "Pardon the pun."

I was relieved to hear most of the girls chortling, and checked the stiff white antimacassar on the headrest of the sofa before taking a seat. Florence read aloud the Bible passage framed beside the grandmother clock.

"'Behold, the day of the Lord cometh, cruel both with wrath and fierce anger. Isaiah 13:9.' Comforting, isn't it?"

I chuckled and read the needlework passage directly below a stuffed screech owl.

"'Happy shall he be, that taketh and dasheth thy little ones against the stones. Psalms 137:9.' We're never going to make it out of here alive," I said.

*

"Ladies, and gentleman." Miss Hazel motioned to a sullen-faced boy leaning against the wall. He reminded me of my brother Christie—long, lean, and a bit scruffy in his canvas work jacket. His dark blond hair was left long on top, parted down the middle, then close-shaved on either side of his head.

"Look at those baby blue eyes," whispered Florence.

"He looks like he knows how good-looking he is," I said.

"We are most happy to welcome you to our humble

home." Miss Hazel read from a clipboard she held up to her spectacles. "I'm sure we will share many—"

"You and your rambling, sister." Miss Tillie snatched the clipboard. She had a mole under her left nostril with three black hairs growing out of it, and I couldn't stop staring. Adjusting the long brown-and-black tail on her coonskin cap, she began. "This is a house of God and will be treated as such. Using the Lord's name in vain will result in expulsion from these premises. You are each and all expected at prayers at six o'clock every morning, and evening vespers at sunset. Sundays are to be spent in silence and prayer. Bath times will be carefully monitored so as to—"

"The hot water's already run out, and it's not even nine o'clock!" a tall girl complained. "How are we to wash?"

"There've been no coal deliveries to these parts since the spring, due to post-war shortages," Miss Hazel explained, although I already knew that. "We have to conserve the best we can until the next coal train comes through. We'll get by, ladies." Her voice sounded reassuring. "With so many of you under our roof, I'm asking you to limit baths to once a week. Here, I've made a schedule so everyone gets a turn. I've added you here at the end, Miss McKenna and Miss Bright."

Miss Hazel put her finger to her lips to silence the girls' protests. I didn't see what the big deal was. Mam only dragged out the bathtub on Saturday nights so we'd all be clean for church, and the water was always growing cold and dirty by the time it was my turn.

"Three inches of tepid, not hot, water for each bath, please. I've marked it on the side of the tub with a grease pen for you."

Miss Tillie gestured toward the boy who was staring down at the floor. "Mr. Will Doherty is one of the new male students here. He's generously volunteered to shovel what little coal remains early each morning to heat the water for our morning washup, and it will be up to you ladies to limit your time at the sink as well as in the necessary room to accommodate everyone. Of course, there's a perfectly functioning outhouse in the back for those of you who—"

"Ugh, I'm going backward," I whispered. Living in the dorm at Haviland had been my first experience with indoor plumbing and a proper toilet.

*

I stared at the empty shelves on the food line in the dining hall. "Creamed chipped beef on toast? Is that it?"

"We have to stretch the food as far as we can," explained Mrs. Bumford from behind the counter. "No one bothered to let the kitchen staff know we have to feed double the number of students we had last year. We couldn't get enough flour, cooking grease, or coffee to make a proper breakfast this morning. Why, we had more food before the war ended." She nodded toward me and smiled, deepening the creases at the sides of her mouth. "Jay, you've grown at least two inches since June."

"Thanks. I don't see the ice cream sundaes. I've been craving them all summer."

"Haven't you heard about the sugar shortage?" she asked. "If it's something sweet you'll be wanting, I tried that recipe in the newspaper for making peach preserves without sugar, but I don't think the girls care for them." She nodded toward a few bowls of overcooked fruit.

"Mam said you need plenty of cow manure to grow sweeter peaches."

"Talking about cow manure on the lunch line? Hayseed." Florence joined me at the cash register.

"How are we ever going to get a seat?" I tried to maneuver my tray through swarms of students packed into seats, leaning against the windowsills, or simply sitting on the floor. "This is insane." It reminded me of my first day at Haviland. Well, not quite. I was alone then.

"There." Florence pointed to a table where some girls were getting up. "Hurry." We weaved our way in and out of the labyrinth of tables until we at last reached the one with a bit of room on the end.

"Look at the boys eating at that back table," I said. "It's nice the way they wear Haviland blazers and ties." I spotted Will Doherty and gave a little wave, but he ignored me.

"He's handsome all right, but arrogant as hell," I said.

"Nah, he's just shy," said Florence. She waved, and Will raised his hand and gave her a shy smile.

*

I awoke in the middle of the night to the smell of sulfur. Someone had struck a match. Who would dare to sneak a smoke at this ungodly hour? Sitting up on my saggy cot, I gasped as I saw a face illuminated by candlelight, staring at me. With dark circles under the eyes, it looked like an apparition.

"Go back to sleep." It was the girl in the bed next to me—the one who slept all day. Her voice sounded ragged and angry.

I swung my feet over the edge of the bed, ready to make a quick getaway. Scanning the rows of beds, I saw no one awake who could help.

"Who are you?" I asked.

"Leave me alone." She held the candle up while she rummaged through a filthy sack she had taken from under her bed.

"What are you looking for? It's the middle of the night, for heaven's sake. Can't it wait until morning?"

"Mind your own business." She slung the sack over her shoulder, blew out the candle, and made her way down the stairs to the main floor and out of the house, shutting the door behind her.

"Where is she going at this time of night?" asked Florence, rubbing her eyes.

I went to the nearest window, where I watched the barking dogs trying to run after the girl. They were all chained to a row of dog houses, so they didn't get far. When the front door slammed again, Florence and I tiptoed downstairs and looked out one of the front windows. I spied Miss Tillie, clad in a wrapper and galoshes, unleashing the dogs. The mangy hounds took off into the misty night, yelping and howling like a pack of wolves.

"Who's trespassing on my property?" yelled Miss Tillie, firing a shotgun into the air.

Terrified, we hid behind the door. Suddenly Will emerged from his bedroom, wearing overalls thrown over his striped nightshirt. Only one shoulder strap was buckled. He ran out after Miss Tillie in his bare feet.

"That's one fine-looking white boy," Florence whispered.

"This isn't the time to be gushing over a boy," I said. "You're going to get us pumped full of lead from Miss Tillie's shotgun if you don't keep quiet."

"Follow the dogs, Will!" she commanded. "There's been an intruder!"

I poked my head out the front door and watched Will take off. Miss Tillie took a few more shots into the night while she waited for the dogs to return. Two cats slithered through my legs out to the yard.

"What in the world? How did you two get out?" She

spied me slinking back indoors. "Get out from behind there right now and explain yourself!"

"We heard gunshots and came downstairs to make sure no one was hurt," I said.

"Did you see the intruder?" she asked.

"No, Miss Tillie," I lied.

Will returned, tied up the dogs, and he and Miss Tillie joined us, tracking mud and wet grass into the parlor. "Whoever it was got away. You can't see anything out there in that fog."

"I'm standing guard for a while." Miss Tillie propped her shotgun up inside the door. "You two"—she pointed to Florence and me with her bony finger—"off to bed, now."

Florence gave Will a little smile. He grinned back at her, grabbed a dish towel to dry his hair, and walked off toward the washroom.

"Did you see the way the blond hairs at his temples were curling into tiny tendrils before he dried them with the towel?" Florence whispered to me as we made our way upstairs.

"No," I said, narrowing my eyes at my friend. Something was up with these two.

"What's going on down there?" Pilar asked, sitting up on her bed.

I stepped quietly over to her so as not to wake the others, but Louise, the girl who lit the cigarette earlier, and Clara, the tall girl, came over to us.

"That girl, the one over there who slept all day." I motioned toward the empty bed. "I woke up to find her going through her bag, and she just left."

"What do you mean, she left?" Louise yawned and pushed her curly, dark hair out of her eyes.

"She just walked out the front door and disappeared. Miss Tillie heard the dogs and started shooting!"

"Shooting?" asked Clara. "I thought the sound was thunder. Did she say where she was going in the middle of the night?"

"No, she just told me to go back to sleep." I felt spooked by the memory of her raspy voice.

"Did you tell Miss Tillie?" asked Louise, grabbing a kitten who snagged its claws on the shawl she had wrapped around her shoulders.

"I didn't want to get her in trouble. Maybe it was some kind of emergency."

"She's up to no good, that one," Pilar said, yawning. "I've got to get some sleep." She rolled over and plumped up her pillow.

I crawled into bed and pulled Mam's fan quilt up to my chin, shivering. It had grown cold as the night air settled in. My bed reeked of camphor balls. Even my quilt had taken on a dank feel. I lay awake, watching bats circling the ceiling until the girl came back with the first pink streaks of dawn. Without a word, she crawled back into her bed.

Chapter Two

Once it became light enough, I studied her face. She looked older than the rest of us, with heavy brows and a slightly upturned nose. Her full lips formed a perfect bow at the center. The indentation between her nose and lips was pronounced. She had deep blue circles under her closed eyes, and her skin was dull and scarred with acne, worse than Evangeline's. Her dark hair was thick and wavy, cut in bangs that curled over her forehead. She didn't breathe heavily or snore like the other girls. In fact, she didn't move at all. She barely looked alive.

I fished around for a facecloth and a cake of soap in my valise and made my way down to the washroom. At least I could be assured of hot water. Not even the old sisters were up, so I thought I'd sneak in a bath just to defy nasty old Miss Tillie. Quietly securing the chain tub stopper into the drain, I turned the ivory faucet marked "H" and watched with disgust as a disappointing trickle of rusty water dripped out. I undressed and sat on the toilet, waiting for the water to reach the line drawn across the side of the bathtub, then jumped up in horror once I felt a cat slinking its way around my bare bottom.

"Get out of here," I hissed way too loudly and scooted the cat out the washroom door.

After soaping up in the tub, I splashed myself with the brown water, brushed my teeth with baking soda, and dried off with my scratchy towel. I sighed as I dressed in my Haviland middy blouse, navy skirt, and black wool stockings. Tying my neckerchief at my collar, I wondered what this school year would bring.

"I can't believe you beat me to the washroom," said Florence as I came out into the kitchen. "I set my alarm clock so I'd be first to get hot water."

"It's rusty-brown, and there's no water pressure," I warned her.

She scooted inside the washroom before any of the other girls could squeeze in past her. There was already a line extending up the stairs.

"Good morning, Josephine," Miss Hazel greeted me from the coffee table in the parlor. "An early riser, like myself. Won't you join me for tea before morning prayers?"

"Did someone have a baby?" I asked, pointing to a light blue bonnet she was knitting.

She stuck her knitting needles into a ball of yarn and placed them in her knitting basket beside her chair.

"Oh, no." Miss Hazel chuckled as she offered me a chintzware teacup and saucer. "These are for Felicity's kittens. The weather will turn cold before the month's out, and I don't want those poor little dears to get chilly. I'm starting on some matching sweaters next."

Convinced that she was completely out of her mind, I made my excuses and proceeded upstairs to dress. When I came back down, Miss Tillie was bookmarking pages in her Bible. Her shotgun was nowhere in sight, and I wondered if last night had been just a bad dream.

After suffering through Miss Tillie singing Fanny Crosby hymns accompanied by Miss Hazel on the tinny piano, I grabbed Florence and took her around the side of the house.

"She came back without a word, at first light," I explained.

"I saw the lump in the bed, but I never heard her come in. Why didn't you tell Miss Tillie she left the house? That nut could have killed someone, firing a gun into the night!"

"They're both crazy. Miss Hazel is knitting a full layette for the kittens. But I didn't want to start trouble on my first night here. That girl must have a good explanation for taking off. I'll ask her the minute I see her."

"I still think you should tell someone, maybe Miss Hazel. She seems harmless enough."

"I need coffee to clear my head before I do anything. Come on, let's go eat."

*

"Is she here?" Florence asked once we found a seat at some extra tables that had been set up outside in the courtyard. "I mean, she has to go to class."

"I don't see anyone here who even remotely resembles the girl who took off last night. She seemed older, but that could have been because of the circles under her eyes."

"She sounds creepy." Florence dipped the last of her toast in the yolk of her egg before standing up. "We've got to get to French now. Didn't you miss old Madame Primrose?"

I caught Florence's arm. "We've got a few minutes before the bell. Sit down. I need to ask you something."

Florence shrugged off my hand and shot me a suspicious look. "What?" Her mouth was set in that straight line that warned me to proceed with extreme caution.

"What was that comment about Will's curly tendrils last night?"

Florence waved off my question with the back of her hand. "He's got nice hair. Don't make something more out of it, okay?"

She grabbed her books and took off to class without waiting for me. I decided to keep my mouth shut on the subject from here on in.

Madame Primrose either needed stronger spectacles, or she was just going senile. She kept checking the time-piece she had pinned to her shirtwaist, even though there was a huge clock on the wall. She clapped her liver-spotted hands to get our attention.

"Ladies, it is past the time that class should begin, so I must insist we get started on our third year of French instruction."

The door opened, and I froze in my seat. I gestured frantically to Florence, who was seated close to me. "That's her."

"You're tardy," Madame Primrose scolded. "Since you are obviously a new student, I'll excuse your lateness today, but you will receive a black mark in my book if it happens again. I'm afraid every desk is occupied, so you'll have to sit at my desk for the present. Can I impose upon one of you ladies to send a message to Mr. Gallagher, the custodian, that we are short one desk?"

Mercy Flanders volunteered, so I had plenty of time to study the girl who had robbed me of a night's sleep. She looked exhausted and unkempt. Her hair hadn't seen a brush in days, and her uniform was too small on her, the buttons about her ample bust threatening to pop open. Her face was probably once pretty, but her skin had a pale, haggard appearance.

"Miss McKenna?" Madame Primrose's mention of my name startled me.

I raised my hand. "Present."

She smiled at me in recognition and returned to her attendance list. "Olive Moody? Miss Olive Moody?"

The girl at the teacher's desk raised her hand without looking up. I thought she might doze off right there in her seat.

Olive never said a word to anyone for the rest of the school day. She caught me staring at her during social studies when her eyes were starting to close. She gave me such an angry glare that I quickly turned away.

After school, I wanted to prolong going back to the attic for as long as possible, so I asked Florence to join me at our special spot by the creek in the woods. A carpet of ochre and crimson leaves muffled our footsteps, and the late afternoon sun filtered through the still-lush copse of maple trees onto the black creek, making it sparkle like so many tiny gems. Water rushed down the mountain from all the rain. I hadn't realized how much I missed the countryside after the hustle and bustle of our summer spent as interns for my friend Ruth Lefkowitz in the state capitol building. Although Florence and I had enjoyed a spectacular view of Albany from the tiny window of the bedroom we shared in a boardinghouse, nothing looked and smelled as good as the forest and our stream off of Lake Gleneida.

"I miss going out on the lunch runs for Al Smith's staff, don't you?" I asked, carefully stepping across the stones in the creek. "We always got lost in Albany and messed up the lunch orders, but everybody was good-natured about our mistakes."

"They were only good about it because they were afraid we'd tell Ruth or Governor Smith on them," Florence said.

"And have you heard from the dashing Charlie Palmer from the governor's office?" I asked.

"I have," Florence answered. "He wants to take me to lunch the next time I visit Mama in Manhattan."

"That sounds serious. He was the most handsome boy on the floor, in case you hadn't noticed."

"You're being generous. He was the most handsome colored telegraph operator out of two working for Governor Smith. The governor had to assure the staff at the capitol that the boys would stay locked away in the telegraph office so as not to make people uncomfortable. That's what Charlie told me."

Although Florence seemed void of emotion as she told me this story, I found myself getting choked up at the humiliation Charlie must have felt. "How could he bear to work under such unfair conditions?"

"He told me he had a choice of either working behind closed doors as a telegraph operator or sweeping the floors with the rest of the black boys," Florence explained. "He took the job that would offer him the most useful experience when he finished high school."

"It seems so unfair. Why were— Never mind," I said, thinking it better not to share what I was wondering. Florence was too quick-thinking to let it pass, however.

"I was treated fairly because I can pass for a white girl," she said. "Charlie and his friend call me 'high yellow.' That's what black people call those of us who can pass for white."

"Doesn't seem fair," I grumbled.

"You just figuring that out now, hayseed?" Florence started skipping stones across the creek.

"So are you meeting him?" I asked.

"I wrote him back and said I can possibly meet him over Christmas break, but that I couldn't make any promises."

"You're a heartbreaker," I said. "The poor boy sent you candy and flowers all summer, and now you're making him wait for you until the end of the whole fall term. He's obviously head over heels for you."

"Charlie is not the only boy in the world, and I'm in no rush to get serious with anyone. Sitting in on those meetings in Ruth's office in Albany opened up a whole new world for me. There's so much I can do for black people, black women in particular, if I do well at Haviland. I don't have to be a maid like my mama. I could work for Ruth or someone just like her to make life better for people like me. I don't want to throw all that away for some boy." She was swirling a branch in the stream.

"And I had to twist your arm to go, remember? I feel the same way. I'm not going to spend my life working myself to death like Mam on a farm, and I'll never chain myself to anyone remotely like my da."

"What about Henry?"

"He wants to expand the family business, modernize it, and he knows I want to be a social worker."

"In Brewster?"

"I don't know. I haven't figured it all out, yet. I know I want to spend a few more summers interning in Albany. I feel so alive when I'm working with Ruth."

"There's some handsome fellows here at school this year. One of them shares a roof with us," Florence teased.

"Will's the biggest snob I've ever seen in my whole life." I snapped the fallen branch I was holding and threw it in the stream. "I tried to catch his attention at breakfast today, just to be friendly, and he completely ignored me."

"Well he doesn't ignore me," Florence said with a mischievous grin. "But then again, I'm prettier than you." She ducked when I threw a handful of wet leaves at her head.

I brushed cat hair off the shoulder of my uniform cardigan. "I'm constantly covered with cat fur. Oh, and speaking of cats, one climbed behind me when I was sitting on the toilet, of all places."

"No!"

"That fleabag animal scared me half to death! That place is an insane asylum."

"We can always stay at my house on the reservoir." She smiled, reminding me that she had inherited the Crane house from her father.

"It must burn Mrs. Crane to no end to hear you say that." I watched some tiny silver fish swimming along with the current of the stream.

Florence's laugh echoed clear through the small glade in the woods.

"Hey, did you hear what Helen Starr was talking about to those popular girls in French?" I asked.

"Why would I care what those idiots talk about?"

"I guess they have special guilds at Haviland, like the sororities you hear about in women's colleges. Juniors are eligible to pledge."

"I don't like where this is going."

The sun was getting low, and the woods grew quiet.

"Helen said you have to pledge, or try out. If the guild is interested in you, they make you do all these crazy stunts to get in, like carrying around a ball and chain on campus."

"It sounds stupid."

"It does. Anyway, they're not officially recognized by Haviland. Plus, no guild is going to want me anyway."

"Well, no guild is going to accept a black girl, so I'm not even going to give it a second thought," said Florence. "It's probably just going to be a bunch of snobs anyway. Who wants to hang around with them? Not me."

"Florence, any guild would be lucky to get you."

She dismissed me with a wave of her hand. "Come on, it's getting late. We'd better go in."

"Oh no, do we have to?" I asked, dreading having to go up to that stinky attic with creepy Olive in the next bed. "Why don't we study in the library? There's no privacy in Fowler House, and we have homework."

*

"So did you hear?" Helen leaned over our table in the library and whispered loud enough for everyone to hear. "I got invited to all four guild teas." She counted off on her fingers: "The Carnation Guild, the Larkspur Guild, the Rose Guild, and the Lily Guild. Nathalia only got one invite, and that's just because her mother's an alumnus."

Evangeline was circling Helen like a shark. I ignored her, pretending to work on math.

"Who cares? They're illegal, remember. Go away, Helen, before I turn you in to Miss Chichester. They're forbidden by her new Anti-Bullying Committee," said Florence, not looking up. She checked her math answers against mine.

"You should care." Evangeline plunked herself down in a chair next to me. "Once you're invited to a guild tea, you're considered popular. If you get invited to pledge, forget it. Everyone looks up to you. And if you get in, well, you're royalty."

"So how many teas have you been invited to, Evangeline?" asked Florence.

"I don't know." Evangeline tried to sound nonchalant. "I haven't been up to the room at all today. Helen, did you happen to see an envelope for me under the door?"

"Nope," said Helen. "They were all for me."

"How do you get invited to a guild tea?" I couldn't contain my curiosity.

"You have to be chosen by the current members to pledge. And if by any chance you succeed in pledging, which very few students do, you become a lifetime member. It's a very selective process, so I wouldn't get my hopes up if I were you."

I gave Helen the snottiest look I could. "You never change, do you?"

She rolled her eyes at me and walked away. Evangeline followed at her heels like an overgrown puppy.

"You can't seriously be interested in all this nonsense," Florence whispered to me once Helen and Evangeline were out of earshot.

"No, of course not. I just want to know why everyone is scrambling for an invitation. I never heard of anything like this last year."

"Sophomores aren't allowed to pledge, that's why," Mercy Flanders explained from the table behind us.

"Ladies, this is a library." Miss Crawford pressed her rubber stamp on an ink pad to mark due dates on a stack of books. "Lower your voices, please."

Mercy ignored her. "Guilds have been going on for generations at Haviland, even though they are not officially recognized. Sororities are really supposed to be only for college girls, but luckily, guilds caught on here."

"What do girls in guilds do?" I asked her, closing my textbook.

"They host teas, socials, and dances, do charity work, and hold fundraisers."

Florence opened my book. "Enough about the dumb

guilds, already. Come on, let's make sure we got the same answers to these math problems."

*

Florence and I were joined by Pilar as we walked from the library toward Fowler House.

"The nights are so quiet up here," Pilar said. "In Key West, you can always hear the water lapping against the anchored boats, and the sweet songs of the cigar rollers when they work late, and the night music of the swamp frogs. There is always music." She started humming softly.

"It sounds like such a beautiful place," I said, dreaming of an island beach, made perfect in my imagination, with pink sand and turquoise water. "What in the world made you want to leave all that for Haviland?"

Pilar's laughter sounded like little bells. "My mother is a Haviland alumnus, Class of '99. She met Papa while her family was vacationing in the Florida Keys. He had just started as a clerk in his father's cigar factory. My mother and her sister wanted to surprise their father with a box of Cuban hand-rolled cigars. My mother said it was love at first sight. They eloped before her family left for home on the steamship. It was quite the scandal, I've heard. She doesn't have much to do with her family anymore, but she insisted I enroll at her alma mater."

"Did you want to leave Florida?" Florence asked.

"No, it was actually my older sister who was supposed to go. She got cold feet and joined the convent just to avoid coming north." She laughed again. "Silly girl. It's not that bad here, and—"

"It's not that bad here?" I asked, incredulous. "We're boarding in the bowels of hell."

30

Her laughter rang out again. "Okay, yes, the accommodations are terrible, but I've never seen such colors." She spread her arms wide as the harvest moon shone over the tops of the ochre- and persimmon-stained maple leaves. "No artist could capture this beauty. Anyway," she said as she flashed me a devilish grin, "as I was saying before I was so rudely interrupted, my papa will be visiting me at least once a month. He's opening five cigar factories in New York. One of them is going to be in Brewster. He's hiring staff up here now. So I won't be that homesick, while my dumbbell sister has to spend the rest of her days as a cloistered nun."

Florence and I laughed and were then entranced by Pilar's tales of the ghosts that haunted the Key West cemetery, Cuban cuisine, and the melodic dances she grew up with, such as the danzón.

As we neared the house, I spotted a lamp burning in what I thought was an abandoned shack. "Someone should put that out before it catches fire."

"It's too far away to be the outhouse," said Florence.

We made our way around the perimeter of the front yard, keeping a safe distance from the barking dogs. Walking toward the outhouse, we came upon an even more dilapidated shack with a door hanging off its hinges.

"Hello?" Pilar asked, barely poking her head inside.

The outstretched claws of a raccoon lunged at us from behind the door. Screaming, we jumped back until we saw Miss Tillie, garbed in work coveralls and a blood-stained apron, running out after us.

"What's the meaning of you sneaking up on me when I'm at work?" She was holding a stuffed raccoon with one empty eye socket in one hand. In her other, she held a glass marble.

"We, uh, just saw the light and thought someone left a lamp burning in the outhouse," I stammered, holding on tight to Florence. "What, uh, what are you doing?"

She summoned to us to come inside. "Get in here and have a look around so you don't come snooping around in my private business anymore."

Once inside the confined space, which smelled strongly of embalming fluid, I observed a bloody work bench covered with knives and tools. Medicine cabinets lined the walls. Hanging from hooks on the ceiling were turkeys, pheasants, a red fox, and several more raccoons. A gun rack was mounted above the door.

"This here is my work studio, ladies. Finest taxidermist these parts have ever seen. Craft handed down from my pa. And I don't take kindly to visitors, so once you've had your fill, leave me to my work and never come back here. You hear me?"

"Yes, we do, Miss Tillie," I said, backing up toward the door. "Nice operation you have here, but we'd best be going now if you'll excuse us."

The three of us ran until we were inside the Fowler House.

"She's as crazy as a loon, that one." I jerked my thumb over my shoulder.

"Who's as crazy as a loon?" asked Miss Hazel. Baxter, the squirrel, was nibbling birdseed off her shoulder.

"Nobody, Miss Hazel," Florence said.

*

"Thank goodness it's Friday," Florence said as we crammed books and weekend assignments into our satchels.

"Ugh, this weighs a ton." I slung my satchel over my shoulder, and Florence, Pilar, and I started down the road from school. As we neared Fowler House, loud popping sounds echoed around us.

"Sheesh! I hear gunshots. We'd better duck," Florence said.

"Miss Tillie's taking target practice to get ready for hunting season, I'll bet." I crouched down low and gave a whistle to announce our arrival to the house.

Miss Tillie lowered her shotgun. "All's clear. Get a move on. This place has been like Grand Central Station today. Folks coming and going all day. Messengers, the girls tell me, delivered two letters. Can't get in a good shot to save my life." She raised her gun and took aim at a rusty tin can. We dropped our satchels and plugged our ears.

After Miss Tillie took a few shots, she paused to reload. We picked up our satchels and scrambled inside the house as fast as our legs could carry us.

"I'll bet there's been an invite for you to pledge a guild, Pilar," I said too loudly, as the gunshot had made me a little deaf. "Your mom is an alumnus, right?"

I started up the stairs but noticed that Florence lingered in the parlor.

"I'm going to the drug store for some penny candy," she said. "See you later."

"I'll come with you," I said. "I don't know what I'm getting so excited about. I don't have a snowball's chance in hell of getting an invite."

Florence motioned with her head toward Pilar. "She wants to share her good news with you. Go. I'll see you later." She checked for gunshots before heading back out the front door.

I joined Pilar and rushed upstairs.

"Where have you been?" asked Clara. "We've been waiting all day to see your Interest Tea invitation."

"Lucky duck, that's what you are. No one else I know got them," called Louise, changing out of her uniform into a day dress.

"Open it, Pilar," I said, rubbing my hands together. "I want to see what one looks like."

"It's not for Pilar," said Clara. "Look, Jay." She pointed to the end of the room by the closet. I spotted an envelope on my cot.

"No, Pilar's mother is an alumnus," I explained. "There must have been a mix-up with the names."

I walked over to my bed and tentatively picked up the square, cream-colored envelope addressed to Miss Josephine McKenna, Fowler House. Carefully breaking the red wax seal, I removed a sheet of cardstock monogrammed with a gold daylily. I read the message in raised black print:

The Lily Guild
requests the pleasure of your attendance
at our annual Interest Tea
to be held on Saturday, October 4, 1919
at 2:00 in the afternoon
at the residence of Mr. Donald B. Austin
on the shores of Lake Gleneida
Carmel, New York

Pilar came to my side, forcing a smile. "Congratulations."

"There must be some mistake." I handed the invitation to her as Louise, Clara, and all the others pushed in to see the delicate, raised calligraphy.

"You're going to be a Gilded Lily!" Louise squealed, hugging me so hard I was sure she cracked a few of my ribs.

"There's going to be no living with you now," said Clara, rolling her eyes.

"Wait." I paused. "Miss Tillie said there were two letters delivered to the house." I turned to Pilar. "I'll bet yours fell under your bed. Let's check."

"Nope." Clara motioned with her head to the bed between mine and Pilar's.

A cream-colored envelope was sitting on top of the lump under the quilt in the bed next to mine.

*

"When do you think Sleeping Beauty will read her invitation?" Florence asked as we changed into our nightshifts for bed.

"Hopefully not at three o'clock in the morning," I said. "I'm sure she has no better chance of being invited to pledge than I do. She's an odd duck."

"Don't sell yourself short, Jay. Everyone knows who you are because you exposed Mary Agnes, and to some degree, Nathalia, for driving Violet to jump out of that plane last year. You never know. Maybe this ridiculous guild wants a hero among their numbers."

"Hero? Hogwash," I snorted. "No one even bothers with me, except you."

"I bother with you, Jay," said Pilar, as she brushed her heavy black ringlets around her finger. "And what's all this about jumping out of a plane?"

"It's a long story." I sighed.

Pilar smiled as she replaced her brush in her valise and settled under her embroidered sheets and coverlet. "I've got all the time in the world."

After relaying the story of Violet's suicide to Pilar, my body surrendered to a sound sleep that lasted for several blissful hours. The black night had wrapped me in silence until well after midnight when I heard an envelope being torn open. I opened one eye to see Olive, illuminated by a flashlight that looked like Mr. Gallagher's, toss the card on the floor. I propped myself up on my elbows. "Why'd you throw that invitation away?"

"Go back to sleep." She turned her back to me and pulled that awful bag of hers up from under the bed.

"What's your problem?" I asked, sick of her rudeness. "You're so nasty."

"Right now, you're my problem." She resumed rifling through her bag. Apparently she found what she was look-ing for because she bolted out of bed and headed toward the stairs.

"Why do you leave at night?" I followed her. "And just so you know, Miss Tillie went after you with a shotgun that first night you snuck out. She thought someone was breaking in the house. She sleeps with her gun. Hope you can outrun her bullets."

Olive's face finally registered a flicker of panic, so I went on. "I never told her it was you, but now I'm thinking I should, because you don't deserve my silence."

"Okay, okay." She put her hands up to quiet me. "I have trouble sleeping at night, because I have a lot going on right now, and I find that taking a walk calms me down. That's where I'm going now, if that's all right with you."

"Nah, you're lying. We all have a lot going on right now. I mean, come on, it's the end of the first week of school, and the teachers piled on tons of homework."

"I mean besides school. I have things to take care of." Her voice trailed off at the end of her sentence.

"Like what? And what in heaven's name are you always looking for in that bag?"

"None of your business, nosy body." Her defensiveness rose up again like high tide.

"Relax, Olive. For Pete's sake, you don't have to be so hostile all the time." I tried to sneak a look at whatever she had snuck into the pocket of her school cardigan, but it was still too dark.

"How do you know my name? I don't know yours."

"We're in all the same classes, silly. And I'm Jay, by the way, Jay McKenna."

"That's a boy's name."

"I wouldn't talk, Olive. That's a vegetable."

"Actually, it's a fruit." And then she actually laughed. As hoarse and dry as it was, it was definitely a little cackle. "Listen, I've got to use the john."

"Thought you said you were going to take a walk." This girl was up to something shady. She reminded me of my sister, Eileen, when she used to sneak out to see Artie.

I was waiting for her when she returned from wherever she had gone off to. "Why'd you throw away that invitation to the Interest Tea? Do you know what most girls would give to be invited to a guild event?"

"Not impressed by all that nonsense." She grabbed her textbooks, which were stacked at the foot of her bed.

"You're not actually doing homework now, are you? And the guilds are not nonsense. Don't you want to meet people? Who knows, you might even like it."

Her greasy hair was plastered to the top of her head, and she didn't smell very good. Picking at the acne scabs along her jawline, she looked at me as if I was a child in need of pacifying. "I told you, I have a lot going on, but if you promise to shut up and let me get my homework done, I'll go to the stupid tea, all right?"

"Deal." Satisfied, I rolled over to try to get a little more sleep. I don't know why this strange girl intrigued me, but she did.

Chapter Three

"Doris and Mae are in room twenty-one, down this hallway," said Helen, her hair still in curling papers. Her face was covered in cream, obviously Evangeline's, based on the rotten stench. "What business do you have with the president and vice president of the Gilded Lilies, and why does it have to be accomplished at the crack of dawn?"

I couldn't resist. Even though it had been sent in error, I waved my invite under her nose. "I received one of these."

Helen's eyes became the size of dinner plates as she rushed down the hall to Nathalia and Mercy's room. I laughed as I heard her shriek, "Wake up! Wake up, you two! You're never going to believe who got an invitation!"

Even if I was only going to be a Gilded Lily invitee for five more minutes, the looks on Nathalia's and Mercy's faces were worth it.

"Hello?" I called softly into the half-opened door of room twenty-one.

Mae Austin, at eight o'clock a.m., looked more elegant than most women did after preparing at their vanity stands all day. Her honey curls were elaborately pinned low at the back of her neck. She wore a lavender embroidered

Japanese crepe lounging robe with a sash belt. "Have we met?" she asked in a voice inflecting the Continental accent politicians and film stars adopted during radio interviews.

I handed her the invitation. "I believe there's been some mistake."

Mae opened the door wider and ushered me into the tastefully appointed dorm room. The walls were covered in Gilded Lily invitations, brochures, photographs, and pennants. Postcards from Europe lined the moldings. She took a seat at her desk and motioned for me to sit on an upholstered ottoman. Reading over my invitation, she asked, "Why do you feel there's been a mistake, Josephine?"

I jerked myself up to full height at the sound of my name. "You know me?" I asked.

Mae's laugh sounded like a gentle spring rain. "I know of you, of course. It's not a very large campus, and you made quite a name for yourself last year, what with—"

I raised my hand to explain. "I'm sorry to interrupt, but you see, a student whose mother is a Gilded Lily alumnus didn't receive an invite, and I assumed there had been a mix-up, as we both are boarding at Fowler House."

Mae took a file from her desk. "How odd. You are correct in assuming that a student whose mother is an alumnus should receive an invite. Let me check our list. Can you provide me with her name?"

"Pilar," I said. "She actually has this big, long, Spanish name that I can't pronounce, but in class she shortens it to Pilar Hoyas."

"I see," said Mae, pausing a few moments before closing the file. "Well, her name's not on the list, and it was just updated last week." She turned to me, folding her hands in her lap. "I'm sorry, there must be a reason for her not being invited to the tea." She then stood up, which I saw as a signal that this meeting was coming to an abrupt end. "Perhaps her mother was not in good standing with the guild, or maybe this"—she glanced at the pad she had written the name on—"this Pilar was misinformed. I would have remembered such an unusual name, and I can tell you with certainty I've never heard of her."

As Mae ushered me out the door, she said, "Unfortunately, some students falsely claim to have a relation who is an alumnus of our guild to gain favor with other students. I'm afraid it's not at all uncommon."

Once I was out in the hall, she added, "I do look forward to seeing you at our Interest Tea, Josephine. It's been a pleasure meeting you, formally, that is."

I stood there, trying to process the flimsy excuse Mae gave me for not inviting Pilar. There had to be more to it. What I couldn't understand was what on earth the Lily Guild wanted with me?

*

I had knots in my stomach. I relayed the reasons, or rather the lack of information, provided to me by Mae Austin.

"She just said your name wasn't on the list, and that there had to be some reason why you weren't invited to the tea. That's all I learned from talking to her."

"Mm-hmm," said Florence sarcastically.

Pilar's voice did not reflect the hurt expression she wore. "Thanks for trying, Jay. Just forget about it. Let's finish all of our homework today so we can relax tomorrow."

We chose the library so we could complete our assignments in peace, away from the damp, crowded attic where frayed nerves from living in such close quarters resulted in petty arguments among the boarders. Turned out every other student had the same idea, so we were constantly interrupted by so-called well-wishers who simply had to congratulate me on my invitation to the Lily Guild Interest Tea.

"Honestly, Jay, I almost fell on the floor when Helen told me you, of all people, were invited to the tea," Evangeline gushed.

"I know, Evangeline. Since they taught us scholarship girls how to read and write, Haviland seems to be going to hell in a handbasket. What will they think of next? Dinner without the required napkin rings or monogrammed bouillon spoons?"

Florence choked on her tea, laughing. Pilar actually spit hers out, soaking her homework page, because she tried holding in her snickers for too long.

"Well, I see some things never change. As Mother says, you can't make a silk purse out of a sow's ear." Evangeline turned and left our table in a huff.

Thankfully, the three of us had more stamina than the rest of the students, so we had the library to ourselves for the final hours of our study session. Miss Crawford, the librarian who had accumulated four pencils stuck in her bun throughout the day, pretended to ignore the tea tray at our table—the one Mrs. Bumford from the dining hall replenished several times over.

Four o'clock found me stretching my arms over my head and flexing my ink-stained fingers to get the blood circulating. "I've got an idea. Let's catch Feenaughty's bus up to Brewster and treat ourselves to root beer floats at Dieter's Confectionary. You know, as a reward for finishing all our work. My treat. What do you say?"

"You want something floating on your root beer?" asked Pilar.

"It's root beer with a scoop of ice cream," said Florence, laughing. "It's good. Come with us. It's not often that Jay offers to pay, so let's take advantage of her guilt while we can."

I shot Florence a snotty look, but as usual, it had no effect on her whatsoever.

I ran up the stairs of Fowler House so we'd be on time to catch the five o'clock bus to Brewster. "Now where did I put my purse?"

I longed for the roomy chifforobe and desk I enjoyed last year in the dorm. Rummaging through layers of dirty laundry in my trunk, I wondered why it seemed that anything I ever needed was always at the bottom. Reaching down into the corner of the trunk, I felt the familiar beaded exterior and gold ball clasp of the change purse my brother Jimmy Joe had brought me back from France when he came home from the war.

"What in the world?" I counted the dollar bills and change. "Hey," I called to Clara and Louise. "Who was snooping around in my things? I had a change purse with over five dollars in this trunk, and now there's a whole dollar missing. Who stole my money?"

"Don't look at us," said a short girl named Eleanor with a towel turban wrapped around her head. "With all of us crammed in up here, who could get away with stealing?"

The other girls nodded, visibly offended.

"You're right, Eleanor. I apologize. I shouldn't have accused any of you. But where could my money be? I counted it three times before I packed this purse."

"Maybe you counted wrong," said Louise.

"No, I made sure I brought enough money to last until Christmas break." I made a vow with myself to find a better hiding place if I was indeed living with a thief.

*

"Oooh, it's like someone carpeted the hills with every shade of yellow, orange, and red."

Florence and I assumed the role of tour guide on the bus as Pilar experienced her first true autumn in the Hudson Valley. The mountains showcased their palette of colors ranging from pale citrine, earthy terra-cotta, rich carmine, to deep aubergine. The cinerous sky provided the perfect frame for God's paintbrush. We got off at Main Street in the village and walked to Dieter's Confectionary.

Seated atop the high swivel chairs with scrolled wrought iron designs on the back, I ordered three root beer floats and two cents' worth of pretzel rods. "I love using the salty pretzel rod to scoop up the sweet vanilla ice cream," I explained to Pilar.

"This smell reminds me of Admiration's Soda Shop in my neighborhood in the city," said Florence as she stuck a red-and-white-striped paper straw in her float.

"Yes, I love the smell of this place, too. What's it a combination of? I can smell chocolate ice cream, tobacco, and what else?" I asked.

"Newsprint," said Florence. "I can smell the ink drying on the typeset in the stacks of newspapers piled up at the entrance." She dipped her pretzel in the ice cream to taste the decadent combination of flavors. "Mmmmm!"

"Newsprint it is," I agreed, savoring the taste of icy root beer.

Mr. Dieter came from behind the cash register and placed the check, which smelled of carbon paper, on our high table. In his thick German accent, he said, "Whenever you're ready, Jay. Take your time, ladies."

"Holy Hannah! This is highway robbery. When did you double the price of the root beer floats?" I asked.

"I'm so sorry, Jay. You haven't been by for weeks, so I can understand why this comes as such a shock. My sugar suppliers are crippling me with their prices since it's in such demand, and I've been forced to pass the cost along to my customers." He spread his hands around the empty shop, save for an old man smoking a pipe at another table. "Business has been bad since the sugar shortage. Tell you what. If you don't have enough, your brothers will be by Monday with the milk and cream delivery. I'm sure they won't mind covering your tab."

"Then you must not know my brothers," I murmured. "I'll pay."

Florence pressed some change into my hand. "Here, Jay, let me chip in."

Pilar did the same.

I shook my head and gave them their money back. "No, I said this was my treat. I've got it. I'm still so sore about someone rifling through my things and taking a whole dollar's worth of the money Mam gave me for canning fruit over the summer."

"My money's on Olive; pardon the pun," said Florence.

"I was thinking the same thing. She's always so hostile, and I wonder what she's up to sneaking out at night. I don't trust her," I said. "Wait a minute." I stood up. "Is that her standing in front of the Southeast House Hotel?" I stepped outside the confectionary to get a better look.

Florence and Pilar joined me at the door.

"I don't see anyone. Where?" asked Florence.

"I could have sworn that was her a minute ago leaning against the building like she was waiting for someone. She must have gone inside. That's weird."

As we made our way back to our table, I asked, "Did I tell you Olive agreed to go with me next Saturday to the Lily Guild Interest Tea?"

Pilar had grown quiet. The elephant in the room had to be acknowledged.

"Pilar," I said, "you should have been invited instead of me. I don't know why—"

"Stop." She put her hand up. "You've been apologizing since you opened that wretched invitation. This is not your fault."

"I just don't understand how—"

"Let it go, Jay." Her voice hardened, which startled me a bit.

Florence looked up from her float. "You still don't understand the way things work, do you, hayseed?"

"What are you talking about? And why are you two ganging up on me all of a sudden?" I pushed my chair back from the table. Sulking, I silently folded my straw over and over until it was no bigger than the tip of my pinkie.

Florence pointed to me as she addressed Pilar. "Explain to her why you weren't invited to the Interest Tea."

Pilar sighed. "In Key West, we stick with our own kind. Cuban Key West is just a, how do you say, an outpost of Havana. We have very little interaction with people outside our community except when we help customers at Papa's stores. He sat me down when Mama insisted I attend her alma mater up north. He told me I wouldn't always be kindly received because we are Cuban, but to always remember that I am a Cuban American, and I have just as much right to be here as anyone else." Her almond-shaped black eyes reflected a fiery pride.

"Wait," I said. "You're telling me that you think you didn't receive an invitation because you're Cuban?"

Pilar nodded. "I wasn't surprised that I didn't receive an invitation. I'm just sad because my mother was a member. I thought that might count for something."

"And you're positive it was the Lily Guild that your mother belonged to?"

Pilar reached under the collar of her middy blouse to reveal a gold chain. Hanging from it was a tiny cross, along with two pendants with miniature pictures of lilies of the valley painted on them. "My mother and my grandmother were members of the Lily Guild. Mama's name was Grace Bailey when she attended Haviland. I never met my grandmother because she and my mother never spoke again once she married Papa and moved to Key West. My grandmother's name was Bernice Simpson when she was a student. I'd be invited if my last name was Bailey or Simpson. It's the Hoyas surname that's a problem for the guild."

"I'm going to straighten this out at the Interest Tea. They can't prevent you from joining if your mother and your grandmother belonged to the guild."

Pilar pushed her float away. "This is too sweet." Getting up, she approached the old man puffing on his pipe at the other table. "May I?" she asked as she gestured to an ashtray on the table.

The old man's watery eyes hung loose in their sockets. He gazed at her, a bit startled at being addressed in such a bold manner by an inferior. He removed the pipe he clenched between his dun-colored teeth and rested it against the ashtray. The corners of his mouth drooped down, disappearing into his matted greyish-white beard.

"I beg your pardon, young lady—that is, if you are indeed a lady. What possible reason would a young woman want an ashtray for?"

"I'm perfectly serious." Pilar smiled politely as she took the ashtray and handed him back his pipe, leaving the old man's mouth hanging open in disbelief. She walked back to our table and took out a cigar from her purse.

"No, Pilar! You wouldn't dare," I said, keeping an eye out for Mr. Dieter.

"I enjoy a nice Havana now and then."

Florence and I watched wide-eyed as Pilar unwrapped the cigar and brought it to her nose to inhale its pleasing aroma. Grinning with satisfaction, she retrieved some contraption from her purse. Clipping one end, she then placed the cigar in her mouth. She struck a match on the heel of her boot and lit the other end, puffing so hard her cheeks resembled those of a squirrel.

"Ah, pure heaven." She leaned back and crossed one leg over the other, blowing smoke rings that smelled like cherries, spice, and the forest. She glanced over at the old man, who was staring, his face further souring into a grimace.

"Dieter!" he yelled to the back office of the store as he stood to put on his hat. "You've seen the last of my business if you're going to allow filthy wetback foreigners in your establishment. You're lucky that I frequented your bakery when everybody else branded you as a dirty kraut during the war, but now you've gone too far."

The bell on the door jingled as he slammed the screen door. He came back in and shook his hat at the frightened shopkeeper.

"And you can be sure I'll tell my brother, Herb, that Dieter allows low-class women to smoke cigars on the premises!"

Mr. Dieter, wearing a pained expression, approached our table. "I'm sorry, ladies. I can't afford to lose any more business. I'm going to have to ask you to leave." He escorted us out the front door.

"But, Pilar, be fair," I said on the bus back to Haviland. "You provoked that old man. I'm not justifying his use of language, but you gave him the shock of his life!" We took turns giving hilarious imitations of his rant.

"I know I did," said Pilar. "But I wanted to prove a point to you, Jay, and I knew smoking a Havana would be the quickest way to get him to show his true colors, the old coot. I do feel responsible for the way he spoke to Mr. Dieter. He seemed like such a nice man."

I clapped my hand over my mouth when I realized why the old man in the store looked familiar.

"What is it?" asked Florence.

"I swore I recognized that old man's face, and I just realized why."

"Who is he?" asked Pilar.

"My brother Packy sells milk and produce to old Herb Bailey at the Brewster House Hotel in the village. Packy mentioned that Herb has a brother who just started as manager at Smalley's Inn in Carmel and wants to use the same milk and bakery providers as Herb, because Dieter is famous for his bread and cake. Your mother's maiden name was Bailey. That means—"

"That you probably just offended your own relation, Pilar!" Florence laughed so hard she started choking again. We smacked her on the back and continued bursting into hoots and hollers all the way back to Fowler House.

Chapter Four

I awoke to the smoky smell of burning leaves. Lacy clouds dusted a robin's-egg-blue sky. I made sure I was first to the washroom to wash my hair, so it had plenty of time to dry before the Interest Tea. I had smuggled bottles of glycerin, potash, borax, and ammonia from the Fowler's kitchen shelf, so I could mix together the shampoo Eileen swore by. Using her recipe, I measured all the ingredients out into a mason jar and poured a third of the concoction over my head, saving the rest for Pilar and Florence. I was scrubbing my scalp the best I could in the brown water when I heard someone pounding on the door.

"I'll be out in a minute." I rinsed my hair, gathered up my things, and made my way into the kitchen, where Pilar was singing some tune in Spanish while pressing shirt-waists in the kitchen.

"Hey, is that an electric iron?" I asked, watching her smooth the wrinkles in a middy blouse laid across an ironing board. "Can I use it when you're done?"

"Sure. It's just like the irons you heat on the stove, only most of the heat is concentrated at this point up front, so you just press the wrinkles out like this." She demonstrated for me. "Just don't get tangled up in this electric cord hanging from the ceiling. This is the only room where I could find an outlet." She then noticed my wet hair wrapped up in a towel. "Today's the Interest Tea. You need to get ready. Why don't you give me the dress you're wearing, and I'll have it pressed for you by the time you finish drying your hair in front of the fireplace."

"You're a lifesaver. I can't decide between two dresses. Can I give you both?"

She nodded as she resumed her singing. She had a nice voice. I wished I could understand what she was singing about.

After an agonizingly long vespers with Miss Tillie threatening our souls with eternal damnation, I spent the rest of the morning dressing for the tea and trying to get Olive to wake up. While Eileen bragged that she had quickly regained her pre-baby figure, she had thrown two dresses in my trunk the day I left for school, claiming that they were hopelessly out of fashion. I smiled when I found they were both fitted in the waist, a body feature I had only recently acquired. Pilar laid both dresses, freshly pressed, across my bed.

"Try them both, and we'll let you know which one suits you best," offered Louise.

I first tried on a sage-green French linen dress, with a white hemstitched collar and an embroidered belt. I nervously stepped from behind Clara's oriental-print dressing screen, our only place of privacy in the attic.

"That looks nice. Let's see the next one," said Clara.

I changed into Eileen's pale-rose net dress finished with lace edges and silk rosettes. "I'd better go with the first one because it's green. Mam says redheads can't wear pink."

"That's an old wives' tale. This dress fits you perfectly and puts some color in your cheeks," said Louise.

That reminded me. I stole a tube of lipstick and a pot of rouge from Eileen's makeup drawer. Did I dare try some today? What if Mae thought I was cheap? I'd better not.

"Yes, definitely wear the pink," said Clara. "I can lend you some pumps if you promise not to break the heels."

I found a cerise grosgrain ribbon Mam gave me last Christmas to wear as a headband. Throwing caution to the wind, I snuck into the washroom and dabbed my finger in Eileen's rouge and smudged the tiniest circle of color on each cheekbone. Clara was waiting with a pair of black, low-heeled pumps with shiny buckles. I thanked her and slipped them on.

"You look nice," said Florence, grabbing her sweater and purse from the kitchen.

"Thanks. Where're you going?" I asked.

"I'm catching a matinee with Pilar, Clara, Eleanor, and Louise at the Cameo Theatre. I've got to go so we don't miss the bus. See you at the lecture later on." She ran to join the group heading outside.

"Oh, okay. Bye." I watched from the window as the five of them headed out onto Gleneida Avenue to catch Feenaughty's bus to Brewster. When did Florence start hanging around with Clara and Louise? What was so great about Eleanor? Why didn't they wait until I would be back from the tea so I could join them? I wiped off Eileen's lipstick with a wet dishrag. It looked stupid anyway. What was I trying to prove, thinking I was Lily Guild material? Who was I fooling? I'd been looking forward to joining Florence for tonight's lecture on the Paris Peace Talks coming up in January. Our history teacher promised extra credit to anyone who attended. What if I got stuck sitting next to Clara or Louise? I didn't even want to go now.

I tried again to wake Olive, but she didn't budge. By noon, I was starting to panic. I charged over to her bed, grabbed the pillow from my cot, and threw it at her head.

"Get up, now! You promised you would go to the tea."

She grumbled a string of expletives that would make Da blush, God rest his soul, and rolled back over to sleep.

"Hey." I shook Olive roughly. "Out of that bed now, or I'll flip it on you."

*

"Listen. I hear music." We approached the manicured lawn of the Austin home along the shore of Lake Gleneida. I spotted a brass quartet playing in a gazebo.

"First, you drag me over here to this godforsaken place, and now you're going to stand there listening to these blessed trumpets all day. Let's get this over with." Olive grabbed me by the elbow and propelled me forward to the slate walkway leading to the white Georgian house with columns.

I peeked inside the black-shuttered windows framed with lace curtains. Several senior girls were seated in the parlor. "This is the place. Here goes nothing." I pulled back the gold knocker and tapped it lightly against the door a few times.

Mae greeted us, wearing a maize silk chiffon frock with flounced layered skirts. "Ladies, how lovely of you to join us. I'm Mae Austin, Senior Sister of the Gilded Lilies." She extended a slim hand that was cool to the touch. "Lovely to see you again, Josephine. Please introduce me to your—"

"Gilded Lilies?" Olive interrupted. "That's ridiculous."

Speaking slowly and deliberately, Mae explained, "That's our pet name for the Lily Guild. The sisters who formed the guild knew we would be teased because Lily Guild sounds so much like Gilded Lily, the name Mark Twain penned to mock the Victorian upper class. They decided to stump the name callers by referring to themselves as the Gilded Lilies. Did you know that our forefathers did the same with the song 'Yankee Doodle Dandy'? The British wrote that song to make fun of us, so to beat them at their own game, the patriots claimed it as their own. Isn't that terribly clever?"

Olive looked at Mae as if she had kangaroos hopping out of her ears. She then turned around and started back out the door again. I grabbed her by the arm and pulled her back in.

Mae continued, unscathed. "Mother offered the use of our home to host this year's Interest Tea." She led us through a cool hallway that smelled of Reflexo furniture polish. Maids garbed in black with white caps and ruffled aprons rushed from the kitchen to the dining room, bearing silver trays heaped with delicacies. "We're just waiting for a few more girls to arrive before we take tea out on the patio since the weather is so pleasant." Her skirts fluttered like angel wings as she swept into the parlor.

I recognized no one as we were introduced to the upperclassmen seated on paisley sofas and Queen Anne chairs. I sat stiff-backed in silence as I took in the elegance of the frosted-glass lamps painted with delicate roses. A black baby grand piano gleamed to a high shine, and a fire was lit in the hearth despite the warmth of the afternoon.

Olive looked out the window, preoccupied with who knows what. She had this disgusting habit of rubbing at the already dry, scaly corners of her lips. She had mastered that fresh-out-of-bed look, having neglected to leave her-self enough time for a proper bath. Eileen's sage-green dress was far too tight on her. The seams bulged under her armpits, threatening to rip if she moved the wrong way. This was not the first impression I wanted to make on the Gilded Lilies.

The front knocker sounded, and Mae rose. "Excuse me, ladies."

I whispered to Olive, "I still can't figure out why I was invited—"

"What'd you stop for?"

"For the love of Lionel, please don't let that be—"

"Don't let that be who?"

"I don't know how you dare show your face around me, Nathalia, after you orchestrated that whole fiasco at last year's Valentine's Dance just to humiliate me." Evangeline, Helen, and Nathalia were led into the parlor. Their entrance reminded me of Cinderella and her two ugly stepsisters.

"And after you kicked me out of my own dorm room," added Helen. "I thought we were friends."

Nathalia had her blond tresses finger-waved to cinema perfection. "I was invited before either of you were. You two just want to ride my coattails to get in, because you know they want me to sing at all their events."

"I'm going." I rose to leave.

"Sit down." Olive yanked on the back of my dress. "You're not going anywhere. You got me into this."

I slumped back into my seat. All the excitement of the invitation had been sucked out of me, like air from a balloon.

"I believe we are all here now, so let's take tea outdoors, shall we, ladies?"

Mae led us through the formal dining room, which opened onto a huge stone veranda. Beyond the yellow-striped awning that hung from the roof, we were afforded a view of the broad lawn leading to Lake Gleneida, glittering in the afternoon sun. The musicians played on. Maple trees of brilliant ruby, ginger, and gold lined the Austin property.

"Real sugar cubes!" I maneuvered little tongs to plunk two precious cubes in a delicate china teacup. "How do you think they've been able to get these?"

"Probably bought it on the black market," said Olive. "That's the only way we'll be able to get hold of booze come January."

"Will you please watch your mouth?" I hissed. "Are you trying to get us booted out of here?"

My stomach growled as I beheld the silver trays piled with herbed cream cheese and strawberry tea sandwiches, smoked salmon toasts, chive-wrapped egg salad sandwiches, and radish tartines. I snuck a finger sandwich from a three-tiered platter and wolfed it down in one bite. I checked my reflection in the polished tea service and picked a piece of watercress from my teeth before anyone saw it.

"What is this red blob supposed to be?" asked Olive, poking her finger into a gelatinous entrée imprinted by a mold with maple leaves.

"Shh. Mind your manners," I scolded, nudging her in the elbow.

"That's tomato aspic, Cook's specialty," Mae explained. "It pairs well with the cucumber sandwiches. Here, Olive, let me spoon a little on your dish, just a taste to try."

"Get that crap away from me." She scraped a layer of cream cheese off of a tea sandwich, which had been cut into a perfect circle. Tossing aside the radish slice, she ate only the bread.

"I'll try some." I handed my dish to Mae while retrieving the errant radish slice with my other hand.

Once we were seated with our tea and savories, Mae first introduced herself as president of the Gilded Lilies and then explained the purpose of the meeting.

"Prospective pledges, you have been handpicked by the Gilded Lilies as possessing the strength, intelligence, and character required to endure the rigorous pledge process. A very select few of you will be invited to pledge. One or two of you, with the necessary perseverance and tenacity, may be chosen as the newest members of the Lily Guild. I'm going to now ask our vice president, Doris Nichols, to explain the good works our guild accomplishes for the school and the community at large."

Doris wore an emerald silk, satin, and velveteen afternoon dress with a loose yoke front and back. Her skirt was trimmed in silk braid and pendant buttons.

"The coveted position of being accepted into the Gilded Lilies entitles you to all the privileges of our guild, for life. We sponsor several charity teas at Haviland, as well as food and clothing drives for the needy of the parish. We will be assisting with the dinner after Thanksgiving Vespers at Haviland, as well as providing refreshments at the Valentine's Day Dance."

Nathalia smiled at me after the mention of the worst day of my life. I shot her a venomous glare.

"Finally," Doris continued, "our June Strawberry Ice Cream Social is our grand culminating soiree. Gilded Lilies sisters are considered campus elite, ladies, and are expected to conduct themselves with the utmost restraint in all affairs, as you are representing our guild in the eyes of our school and the community at large."

"How'd you pick people?" asked Evangeline. "I mean, of course you picked me because Mother was a Gilded Lily, but"—she waved her hand toward me—"why'd you invite these other girls who have no family connections?"

I imagined dumping the tomato aspic over Evangeline's head of unraveling sausage curls.

"You have a problem with who was picked?" Olive stood up from her chair and charged at Evangeline. Nose to nose, she threatened, "Because if you do, we can settle it outside."

For the first time since I'd met her, Evangeline backed down, speechless. I stared at Olive, not knowing what to say. Why was she so volatile? She reminded me of a tiger ready to pounce at the slightest provocation.

As cool as the paper-thin slices of cucumbers in the sandwiches, Mae addressed Evangeline's question.

"You are correct, Evangeline, that students whose mothers are Gilded Lilies alumni are invited to our tea, but that alone isn't a guarantee that you will be invited to pledge."

I heard Nathalia whisper, "Yes, it is," into Helen's ear. "If your mother was a Gilded Lily, you're in."

I'd had enough of this. I stood up and addressed Nathalia loud enough for Mae and Doris to hear. "No, apparently having a mother and a grandmother who are both Gilded Lily alumni doesn't guarantee an invitation if your last name is Hoyas."

Mae approached me, smiling. Taking my hands lightly in hers, she led me into the hallway.

"I did try, Josephine, to follow up on our conversation, truly I did. I'm afraid my search for your Miss Hoyas proved fruitless."

"That's impossible," I argued. "Pilar showed me the Gilded Lily charms that belonged to her mother and grandmother. Their maiden names were Bailey and Simpson when they attended Haviland. Isn't that American enough for membership?"

In a voice that dripped honey, she replied, "You're mistaken about our requirements, Josephine. We're quite the eclectic group. Why, Doris's mother was raised in India."

I stifled a laugh at her attempt to prove the Gilded Lilies' diversity and followed her back into the parlor. "Let me guess. She's British."

Mae stuttered a bit. "Well, yes, but India is a very exotic country. Elephants and spices, that type of thing."

"Students are recommended to us as good prospective pledges based on character, which we consider as, if not more, important than having a relative who is an alumni," Mae continued, pausing only to take a sip of tea. "Students who have triumphed in the face of adversity, who have contributed to Drew Seminary, and who have been an example to others are the girls we want as Gilded Lilies."

I thought about last year: the bullying, figuring out that Mary Agnes drove Violet to her suicide, and the formation of the bullying prevention committee. Could someone have possibly recommended me to the Gilded Lilies?

"Prospective pledges, we invite you to enjoy some desserts now while the Gilded Lilies take care of some business. Invitations to pledge will go out by the end of the week." Mae led the others through the French doors into the dining room.

"Which one of you is Olive Moody?" Nathalia asked, selecting a raspberry cream tart from a tower of miniature pastries.

"Who wants to know?" asked Olive, wrapping some éclairs in a napkin. She quickly shoved them in her bag before turning around.

Nathalia took a step back. "My mother asked me to find out."

"Why?" said Olive, eyes narrowed.

"She needs her mother's address; um, that is, she wants to send an invitation to her, and I guess, you, to the Gilded Lilies Alumni Mother–Daughter Tea. Mother's chairwoman of Alumni Committee this year," said Nathalia.

Olive shot her a menacing sneer. "Why would she invite my mother to a tea?"

Nathalia struggled to decode the invitation she took from her purse. I recalled how she tried to hide her illiteracy from the teachers during our sophomore year. "Mother specifically told me to find out her address. Here, Jay, you read it. You brought this person here."

I took the note from her. "Mrs. Ethel Moody, Gilded Lilies, Haviland Class of 1899. Your invitation came back in the mail, marked 'Return to Sender.'"

Nathalia snickered. "Didn't you even know your own mother was a Gilded Lily? How unusual."

Olive wavered momentarily before grabbing the invitation from me. "Of course I know my mother is an alumnus." She charged Nathalia. "Are you saying I'm dimwitted?"

Nathalia, eyes widened in terror, fell backward into a chair. "Helen, be a dear and fetch me a cup of weak tea. I'm feeling a bit woozy."

Olive shoved the invitation in her bag. "She can't go. She's been, uh, unwell. And I'm not going either. I have more important things to do than sit around making small talk with a bunch of snooty old ladies."

Nathalia sat silent and red-faced. Helen brought her tea before going off into a corner to whisper with Evangeline.

"Is this thing almost over?" Olive asked.

I'd never seen someone whose mood could change at the flick of a switch. Yes I did. Da used to get like that.

Olive downed the rest of her tea in one swig. Wiping her mouth with the sleeve of Eileen's dress, she stood up. "I've had enough of these windbags. Let's get out of here." She trudged through the house, past the senior sisters, and out the front door.

Nathalia approached me. "You keep that trash away from our meetings, Jay McKenna. She doesn't belong, even if her mother was a Gilded Lily."

"I didn't bring her," I said. "She was invited, just like the rest of us."

By the time I said my goodbyes and made my way out to Gleneida Avenue, Olive was gone. Unfortunately, Evangeline and Helen were not, as they had left at the same time I had. I tried to walk quickly to lose them, but I knew they were trying to keep step with me so they could gossip about Olive.

"Wonder where she went off to?" I shielded my eyes and looked toward the center of town. In the distance I spotted Olive talking to a rough-looking guy in a newsboy cap in front of the Carmel Drug Store. I ran toward her.

She met me halfway. "You go on back. I've got things to do," she said, almost out of breath. "I'll meet you back at school."

A vein started throbbing on her forehead as I stood my ground, arms crossed.

She shoved me and yelled, "Well go on now, scram!"

I looked suspiciously at the guy in the cap, leaning against the storefront. "What things, Olive? We have to be at the lecture at six so we get extra credit in history. You didn't do so hot on the first test, remember?"

"Mind your own damn business." She turned and ran back to the drug store.

"What is it with that one always running off?" I asked Evangeline and Helen. Unfortunately, I couldn't avoid walking back to campus with them. My only solace was that Nathalia had stayed behind to learn the Lily Guild's official anthem.

"I don't know, but why is she always so irritable, ready to bite someone's head off all the time?" Helen asked. "She's got to show better manners around those guild girls, or she's never going to get in, no matter who her mother is."

"Wonder what she's talking to that sketchy-looking guy about," I said. "I don't even know where she's from."

I walked in silence for a while, taking in the magenta hues of the maples reflected on Lake Gleneida and ignoring Evangeline's rambling about how she was perfect Gilded Lily material while I shouldn't be disappointed if I didn't receive an invitation to pledge. Once I could bear it no longer, I told them I had to get ready for the lecture, even though I had plenty of time. I sprinted ahead the rest of the way.

*

"Hey, wait for me!" I shouted when I spotted Florence coming down the steps from Fowler House. "Did you forget something?"

"You're kidding me, right?" Florence kept on walking.

I caught up to her and grabbed her arm. "What's wrong? We were supposed to meet here at six o'clock for the lecture."

She shook her arm free of my hold. "Five o'clock, Jay. The lecture's over. Listen, go back to your tea party with Nathalia, okay?"

"My stars, I got the time wrong. I was just so nervous about the tea, and it was so important and all. Let me make it up to you, please? Can we at least have dinner together and study for math?"

Florence stopped, glaring at me with those bottle-green eyes. "Pilar invited me to join her and the others for the lecture, followed by dinner in the dining hall and going over our notes from the lecture afterward in the library. I turned them down because I explained that you and I were going to sit together, have dinner and study afterward like we always do on Saturday nights. I saved you a seat for the lecture, and I ended up sitting alone, away from my friends who can tell time and have their priorities straight. Maybe if I hurry I can catch up with them. Go sit with Nathalia and Evangeline for dinner." She walked away.

"Fine." I stood there, alone, as Florence headed up to the dining hall. I couldn't prevent the tears that I had been able to hold back this morning from falling. I'd lost her. The best friend I ever had was gone. And it was all my fault. I kicked a stone back to Fowler House, utterly disgusted with myself.

*

THURSDAY, OCTOBER 9, 1919

I couldn't watch Florence laughing at Clara and Eleanor's table for one more dinner. I dumped my tray and stormed out of the dining hall, gulping back tears of loneliness and frustration. Florence had been polite but distant this entire miserable week. Invitations to pledge weren't even out yet, and I was already growing tired of the constant bevy of girls going on and on about their need to be a Gilded Lily. I missed my friend. I dragged myself upstairs and tried to figure out my math homework, alone.

Around midnight, I gave in to my fatigue and quit my books. It was hard studying without Florence. I wanted to talk, but she was sleeping with her back facing me. Not bothering to undress, I pulled my quilt over my head to drown out the nose-whistling snores from the rows of girls. Olive was nowhere to be seen. I felt like I used to with Eileen, like a mother hen worrying about her where-abouts. I fell off to a burdened sleep, worrying about Florence leaving me to fend for myself in this school and Olive being lured into a life of crime by undesirables.

I heard a stone thrown against a window. I bolted upright, thankful to wake from the terrible nightmares I had been suffering through as I slept. I'd dreamt of Violet, open-eyed and broken as I found her that day by the stone wall, warning me to be wary. What did that mean?

Another stone pelted against the window. The latch was rusted shut, so I jiggled it as best I could until it gave a little. With all my strength, I pushed the rickety pane upward, paint chips falling down on my hair and my nightshift.

"What's all that racket?" asked Florence, joining me at the window.

"Get down here, now!" It was Will. I could barely make him out in the moonless night.

"No." I tried to keep my voice to a loud whisper. "It's the middle of the night. We'll get in trouble."

"Come down here this instant!" Will looked about ready to pop a blood vessel.

Going outside at this hour to meet a boy we barely knew did not seem like a good idea at all. However, Will didn't seem like he was looking for a midnight rendezvous.

Florence and I tiptoed as quietly as we could past the rows of sleeping girls, sidestepping piles of dirty laundry. I felt around with my bare feet for sleeping cats or squirrels as we made our way downstairs into the parlor. Once I silently unlocked and turned the doorknob to the front door, we got down on our hands and knees and crawled through the wet, moldy leaves so as not to wake the dogs. It didn't work. One hound started howling at the sound of crunching leaves, and he got the others barking. We were crouched under Miss Tillie's bedroom window when I saw the reflection of a flickering flame in the glass. She had lit her lamp. I heard her use the good Lord's name in vain. I guessed she must have stubbed her toe or tripped over a cat.

We got up and ran for dear life around the back of the house to warn Will.

"Hide! Miss Tillie's coming with her shotgun." We hit the ground and elbowed our way back toward the outhouse, where we crouched down and hid. Will followed us.

"Why did you call us down here? We're going to get shot full of lead!"

Panting, Will jerked his thumb toward the outhouse. "I had to make a trip out here, because, you know, I had to go; and I found one of your fool friends passed out. Get her out of there and back into her bed, now, before Miss Tillie kills us!"

At the sound of the first shot, he pushed my head down into the septic mud leaking from the faulty outhouse. Stifling my gag reflex, I remained motionless until I heard Miss Tillie reprimand the dogs and slam the front door shut behind her.

"She's gone," Will whispered. He had covered Florence with his body to shield her from Miss Tillie's gunshots. "Now help that darn girl out of there."

The door to the outhouse creaked open when I pulled on it. Will held up a lantern, revealing Olive leaning against a stack of newspaper squares. She must have nodded off while in a standing position. I breathed through my mouth so as not to take in the stink of the place while Florence shook her awake. She mumbled a few choice swear words while Will and I each took one of her arms and draped them around our necks. She staggered a bit but allowed us to drag her out into the yard.

Together we managed to drag her a full six feet before the dogs started up again. We froze at the crack of Miss Tillie reloading.

"Run for it!" We dropped Olive in the wet leaves and headed around the back of the house, only to face the barrel of a shotgun when Miss Tillie ambushed us at the corner.

"What on earth is going on?" Miss Tillie motioned with her gun for us to back up, hands in the air where she could see them.

"It's Olive, Miss Tillie," I said. "She must have fallen asleep in the outhouse, and Will threw pebbles at the window so we would come down and help him get her back to bed."

"Well, where is she?"

"Over there." Florence motioned. "We'll bring her inside if you put the gun down."

"Well, be quick about it. I haven't slept a wink."

"Jesus, you weigh a ton," said Will as we hoisted Olive up, leaves sticking to her clammy skin.

"Mercy me. She hasn't come down with the flu, has she?" Miss Hazel appeared in a red flannel nightgown, buttoned up to her chin. She must have put the kettle on the stove top while we were running for our lives.

Will unceremoniously deposited Olive on the sofa. I rushed to take the whistling kettle off the flame so as not to wake anyone upstairs.

"There hasn't been a case of the flu around these parts for the better part of a year, sister," said Miss Tillie. "She looked passed out drunk if you ask me, but I don't smell any liquor on her breath."

"Leave me alone, for Lord's sake." Olive pushed away the cup of tea I offered her, splashing scalding water on my hand.

I bolted to the sink and pumped cool water over my blistering skin. "We should have left you out there to rot."

"I've seen the flu come on without a minute's warning," Miss Hazel persisted. "I'm thinking you should go home for a few days just to be on the safe side. We don't want you exposing the whole house to whatever infectious disease you've managed to contract. Do you have family close-by, Miss Moody?"

"No. I told you, I'm fine. I'm just tired."

"You're always tired," I said, shaking the pain out of my hand.

"Miss McKenna, could you bring Miss Moody up to your farm, just for the weekend, to make sure she's well? I'm so afraid of her infecting the other girls."

"But it's fine for her to infect my family, is that it?" I asked, incredulous. "My brother—" I stopped. Christie's death was none of their business. "I don't know. I'll have to think about it." Boy, had this been a lousy day.

"Some fresh air and rest might be just what Olive needs to put some color in those cheeks. I heard you discussing how you were visiting home this weekend." Miss Hazel's smile made my teeth hurt.

"It would be the Christian thing to do," added Miss Tillie.

"I said I'll think about it."

"You may use our telephone to call your mother in the morning and ask permission if you'd like," said Miss Hazel.

"You have a telephone?" Florence asked.

"I warned you not to say anything about that, sister," scolded Miss Tillie. "Now they'll all want to use it, and we'll end up in the poorhouse."

"It couldn't be much worse than this dump," Olive muttered as she stumbled up the stairs.

I couldn't be sure, but I thought I spied the sides of Will's lips turn up in something akin to a smile when Florence bid him a good night.

Chapter Five

Serenaded by the clip-clop of old George and Martha trudging up Brewster Hill, I rested my head on Henry's shoulder, savoring the feel of his flannel work shirt, warm against my cheek. I inhaled the scent of apples rotting in the autumn sun, a feast for the last of the yellow jackets. I tried to name all the colors of the mountains as we turned onto Brewster Hill. The maples ranged in shades from butternut to scarlet. The baby-blue sky was exploding into violet and fiery orange at the western horizon. I was in the middle of a painting that no human could capture with the perfection that surrounded me.

"Want to grab a movie later on?" he asked. "You look amazing, by the way." The sugar shortage had had a positive effect on my figure.

My cheeks colored at the compliment. "So do you. I've been dying to see *True Heart Susie* with Lillian Gish. I think it's at the Cameo."

Henry made a sour face. "I wanted to see *The Lost Battalion*."

"Next time, I promise."

I turned around in my seat and tried to rouse Olive. She was out cold, sprawled on top of Henry's feed sacks. "Wake up. We're here."

I waved to Felix and Ernie, our farmworkers who were finally back with us full-time. Ernie was repairing a hole in the roof of the barn. I counted four new cows in our paddock. While everyone else was struggling with shortages since the war ended, Jimmy Joe and Packy were somehow pulling our farm out of the red. Felix was stacking crates of apples and turnips in the truck for delivery to Frank Maher's Greengrocers in the village.

"Do you really think your friend is coming down with the flu? I thought we were done with that whole nightmare." Henry took my valise and satchel down from the cart. "She certainly looks like death warmed over."

"No, she doesn't have the flu. She always looks like that. There's something not right with her, but I can't figure out what it is. I hope Mam's going to be all right with Olive staying. I let the telephone ring forever but no one picked up." I went ahead to the porch to prepare my mother for our odd guest, only to have Sullivan leap from the top step into my arms, knocking me backward.

"Oh, my precious baby!" I wrestled with my dog in the leaves before getting up and helping Henry carry my things into the house.

Once we were outside again and past the kitchen window, Henry curled his fingers around my face and pulled me in for a long, warm kiss. The coarse hair above his lip scratched the skin around my mouth, but I pulled him closer to me.

"I've looked forward to that for over a month." He smiled as he held my face in his hands before giving me three more short, sweet kisses.

"I like the mustache." I brushed it with my fingers. "It tickles, but it makes you look like Douglas Fairbanks."

"I'm shaving it off then. That guy's a drunk." He laughed.

I hugged him tightly before ruffling his mop of blue-black hair sitting atop the shaved sides and back of his head, similar to Will's haircut. "You have much better hair than Douglas Fairbanks, especially cut like this."

"Thanks. I'll be by around seven with the truck if my dad lets me take it."

"Help me get this one down and onto the porch," I said as I climbed up onto the rig and roused Olive.

"Where the hell are we?" she growled as we helped her from the rig.

"My house, and if you know what's good for you, you'll keep your mouth shut and do what my mam tells you to," I growled back at her.

Henry grabbed the reins and guided George and Martha back out onto Brewster Hill.

I scooped up Sullivan and waved to Henry until he was out of sight. I touched my lips and cheeks, still feeling his touch on my skin. I was looking forward to more of his kisses later on during the movie. Now, however, I had to contend with explaining Olive's presence to my mother.

"Another mouth to feed with barely enough for the rest of us? And sickly as well, with a baby in the house?" Mam sliced a potato and added it to the onions and apples she was frying in a cast iron pan. "Josephine, your timing couldn't be worse, what with Christine colicky, and all the work that has to be done tomorrow. The two of you will have to sleep in the parlor, but not if she shows any signs of the flu. I'll not have her infecting this house."

"I called, but you never answered the telephone. Why can't we sleep in my room?" I watched her put the kettle on and grab the hot water bottle she kept under the sink. Olive would receive better treatment from Mam than she would at any hospital, even though I doubted she was sick.

"Before you start complaining, I'll have you know I moved into your room with Eileen and the baby so Packy and his wife can have my room. It's closer to the washroom for him with his wooden leg, poor fellow."

I noticed she didn't refer to my new sister-in-law, Nancy, by name.

I went into my room to look for warm pajamas, only to find my dresser drawers crammed with baby clothes. I could barely make my way to the overstuffed closet with baby Christine's cradle and the stinky diaper pail in the way. I guess I didn't live here anymore.

"She's an odd duck, that one," Mam whispered, pointing to Olive on the sofa as I came out into the parlor. "Not a sick bone in her body. Hungover, if you ask me. She gave vague answers as to where her kinfolk live. I don't trust her as far as I can throw her. I'm hiding your da's gold pocket watch."

I shrugged off her suspicions, except they got me wondering about my missing money.

"Josephine, tend to the baby while I finish slicing these tomatoes. Olive, you don't look like a good Catholic. I'm thinking you're a left footer like the rest of those Haviland girls. There's no meat served in this house on Friday, so you'll have to do with these potatoes and fried lake trout my poor, one-legged son caught this morning in the Sodom creek, God love him. Get off the couch and fill everyone's glasses with milk. My good, strong boys will be in for their supper any minute."

I scooped up the wailing baby Christine from a pile of quilts surrounded by sofa cushions on the floor in the parlor. While she was named for my late brother, I swore I was looking at Artie Tuttle's face attached to a five-month-old baby's body. I burped her to bring up some gas. "Where's

Eileen?" I asked Mam once Christine let out a satisfying belch.

Mam waved me off. "Don't get me started. She's looking for work in that new cigar factory that's opened up in the village. Milano's Dressmakers won't take her back on account of the baby, and I don't blame them. She should be home taking care of her daughter. A cigar factory! Can you even imagine your sister rolling cigars? Olive, wash that pimply mug of yours before supper. And stop scratching them. You'll get permanent scars. I'll drag out the tub and we'll heat some water for a bath. You look like you could use a good scrubbing."

I laughed at Mam's crassness, for it resulted in Olive's meekly doing as she was told. Christine had been soothed to sleep, so I laid her back down on her makeshift crib in the parlor before bringing out the bowls of fried potatoes, along with a dish of corn relish and some pickled cucumbers to the supper table. Olive helped herself to a biscuit before Mam grabbed the plate from her.

"Wait for my sons. They've worked hard all summer to put all this food on the table."

Startled, Olive muttered, "Sorry, Mrs. McKenna."

Jimmy Joe ducked as he came in from bringing the cows in for the night. Felix and Ernie followed behind.

"Put on clean shirts for supper, the lot of you." Mam set a cup of tea in front of Olive. "Drink this. It might bring back some color to your face."

Sullivan came through the dog door Jimmy Joe had installed and ran to the table to look for any food that might have fallen on the floor. He jumped up on Olive and sniffed her.

"Get this mutt away from me," she growled.

"Don't you like dogs?" Jimmy Joe smiled at her. He had changed into a light blue oxford shirt and had combed his hair back. Even with his face and ears burned in the war, he had a smile that should have been in a tooth powder advertisement.

For once, Olive didn't have a nasty comeback. "They're okay, I guess."

"You need to learn to be more pleasant as a dinner guest." He flashed another grin at her before downing his glass of milk in one gulp and wiping his mouth on his sleeve.

"Look who's talking," she teased, handing him her table napkin. "You need to learn better table manners."

"What are you doing?" I hissed.

"Nothing." She giggled.

"Well, just stop it."

"Relax, Jay. I'm just being friendly."

This was not the Olive I knew from the attic. What the hell was going on here?

"Oh dear, let me get the door for Packy." Mam moved the black cast iron pan with fried trout to a cooler part of the stove top and raced to meet my second brother, who was planting his cane to steady himself. He gingerly moved his wooden leg inside the kitchen, using his good leg for leverage. His new bride, Nancy, waited patiently behind him so he could enter the house on his own.

"Take my arm, son, and let me help you inside," said Mam.

"That's a lovely gesture, Mother McKenna, although as you know, Padraic can manage." Nancy Outenhausen McKenna, having just finished her rounds from Florence Shove's District Nursing Association in the village, was dressed in her smart blue wool cape and hat secured by hair pins. Her straight skirt fell to midcalf, above dark stockings and low-heeled pumps.

Packy and Nancy were physically a study in contrasts. While my brother's blond locks were still shorn close to his head, marine style, Nancy's thick, dark chocolate curls seemed hastily cut to chin-length, reminiscent of Jo March when she sold her hair in *Little Women*. Packy's eyes were light cerulean like Mam's, while Nancy's dark russet eyes, flecked with gold, shone brightly with intelligence. Her narrow Roman nose, sharply sculpted cheekbones, and dark, full brows reflected strength and confidence.

Ignoring Nancy, Mam removed Packy's jacket and leaned over to take off his work boots before offering her arm to guide him to the supper table.

Nancy maintained a strained smile and asked, "Is the kettle still hot? I just want to change before I enjoy a restorative cup of tea. I had nine home visits today plus a full house at the clinic, and I'm about ready to drop. My, that food smells good. I'm famished."

"I'm sure my poor, crippled son is exhausted, too, after a full day of managing the books and negotiating deals with our creditors, not to mention driving you home from work. Maybe he would appreciate his wife fixing his tea first." Mam spoke through her gritted teeth.

I stood up. "Go change out of your work clothes, Nancy. I'll bring you and Packy tea."

She looked at me as if I just threw a life jacket to her while she was trying to swim to safety from the *Titanic*.

"Packy, you may say grace tonight," said Mam as she took her place next to him.

"The Crowned Prince Padraic," whispered Jimmy Joe to Olive, causing her to erupt in another fit of snickers. What in the name of all that's good and holy was going on?

"I'll just be a minute, Mother McKenna. Please wait to say grace until I sit down, won't you?" Nancy maintained steady eye contact with Mam.

"As you wish, although I know no Protestant prayers, and it would be a shame for my boys to eat cold potatoes after a hard day's work in the fields."

A few minutes later, Nancy emerged from Mam's former bedroom, wearing one of Packy's old sweaters and what looked like a pair of men's trousers. I was instantly impressed.

"That hardly seems like proper dining attire, Nancy," said Mam.

"I love them," I said. "I want a pair."

"These were all the rage at Endicott Hospital in London where I served with the Red Cross before being transferred to the base hospital in France. Actually, two American volunteers, Marian Dickerson and Nancy Cook, wore them during our breaks, and they just caught on. They're just so much more practical than skirts."

"Well I suppose if you want to go around looking like a man, that's your business," said Mam.

"I agree with Nancy. I think they're practical and comfortable, and I'm going to buy a pair as soon as I can afford them," I said.

Nancy mouthed a silent thank-you to me before bowing her head as Packy began with, "Bless us Our Lord, and these thy gifts, which we are about to receive, from thy bounty, through Christ our Lord, Amen."

"Rub a dub dub, thanks for the grub, yea God, yea God!" shouted Jimmy Joe before busting into laughter along with Olive. "Now listen here, everybody, especially you two," he said, pointing to Felix and Ernie. "We'll not be selling any more cider apples to Frank Maher this harvest season. Stack up the crates in the root cellar. We'll be needing every apple that falls from our trees."

"But, son, haven't you been reading the papers?" asked Mam, passing the fried fish to Packy. "They're full of ads willing to pay good prices for cider apples."

"And why do you think that is?" asked Jimmy Joe. He flashed his most devilish smile, chock-full of big white teeth.

"I've no idea. I just think it's foolish not to take advantage of any opportunity that will make us money."

"Of course everybody and their brother wants to get their hands on as many cider apples as they can. Prohibition's coming in January. There'll be no more liquor served or available for sale anywhere—"

"That's not entirely true, Jimmy Joe," Nancy interrupted. "Doctors can prescribe alcohol for medicinal—"

"Oh, will you hush up and let the man finish!" scolded Mam.

"Anyway, as I was saying, we have the opportunity to quench a national thirst come January, and we have the means to do so growing on our trees!"

"Applejack?" asked Packy.

"Yes, applejack." Jimmy Joe nodded. "And people are going to be willing to pay any price to quench that thirst, right? Plumbers all over the county are making money doing the pipework for stills that are popping up in every barn as far as the eye can see. We can go that route if we want to, of course, but we've got a goldmine sitting in those crates out in the truck. Why should we sell them now just so others can make money? Felix, Ernie, take those crates down from the truck and start making room in the cellar for them right now."

"You got it, boss. Right away." Ernie grinned at my brother's entrepreneurial foresight.

Mam pounded the handle of her knife into the table to command order. "I'll not tolerate talk of any enterprise involving the illegal sale of alcohol at my supper table." She reminded me of Miss Tillie. "Now hush your talk and pass your plates to me so I can soak them while I put out the tea and cake."

"Now look what you've done," I said, as we heard a new round of wails from Christine. I filled a baby bottle with milk and warmed it in a pot of water on the stove.

"She's too young for cow's milk," said Nancy. "Where's Eileen?"

"Out looking for work," said Mam. "We know what we're doing, Nancy. I raised five children, may I remind you?"

Nancy left the table and joined me in the parlor. "I'll change her if you want to watch the milk so it doesn't get too hot. The cow's milk is probably what's giving her colic. She's too young to be weaned off the breast."

"I'm sure you're right. Eileen should be here." I left to test the heat of the bottle while Nancy picked up Christine and nuzzled her against her neck. "Let's get you out of this wet diaper. There now, Aunt Nancy's here."

Christine was soothed by her nurturing voice, and snuggled into her embrace, her fists relaxing.

I squeezed the nipple of the bottle onto my arm to check its temperature before bringing it into the parlor to feed Christine. Nancy handed me my niece and we settled on the couch for a good feed.

Nancy came out of my former bedroom with the full diaper pail. "These soiled diapers have been sitting way too long. They're covered in flies, which is unhygienic. We have to soak them overnight in bleach to get them clean."

"Here comes Florence Nightingale again, even though she's never had a baby," said Mam. "Give them here. I'll take care of them."

"No, I'll do it," I volunteered, even though my stomach lurched at the prospect. "Nancy, would you feed her?"

Nancy's gratitude radiated throughout her entire face.

Once the kettle was singing, I filled a washtub out on the porch with hot water, bleach, and some soap flakes. Holding my nose, I dropped the soiled diapers in the tub and rubbed them against the washboard. Mam could feed them through the wringer later on after they were bleached white again. It was at this time that Henry decided to drive up in the Harkin's Feed and Supply Store truck. He was wearing a clean pinstriped shirt and dark wool vest, a small gold ball securing his stiff, new collar. I reddened as I realized the sorry state he had found me in.

"Oh, Henry, give me a minute to change." I left the diapers to soak, ran inside, and tore through my valise, looking for something clean.

Nancy looked up from the sofa where she was feeding Christine. "I have another pair of trousers that may fit you."

"Really? Would you actually lend them to me?" I asked, delighted.

"Sure. Take the baby for a minute." She rose and handed a satiated Christine to me.

"Josephine, let Henry in out of the cold, for goodness sake! Where are your manners?" Mam called as she spread a thick layer of butter on slices of soda bread for Jimmy Joe and Packy.

I brought the baby to the door and opened it for Henry. "Would you be a dear and hold her just a minute?" I asked as I dumped poor Christine unceremoniously in his arms. "I'll just be a second."

Mam flew at Henry like a turkey vulture claiming its prey. "For the love of God, give me that child!" she screeched, wrenching the baby from his sturdy embrace. I slinked into my former bedroom to the echoes of her admonishments about babies being women's work, not men's.

"What in heaven's name are you wearing?" she shrieked when I emerged in Nancy's khaki trousers.

"It's almost 1920, Mam. We have to move with the times."

"Where do you think you're going?" asked Jimmy Joe.

"Henry's taking me to the movies in his dad's truck."

"Are you seeing the new Lillian Gish movie?" asked Olive.

"Want to go?" asked Jimmy Joe. "I'll take you."

"You've got to be kidding me," I said, shooting Henry and imploring look. "We haven't seen each other in a month."

"Stop being a spoiled baby, Josephine," said Mam. "Jimmy Joe fought in a war while you were at your fancy girls' school. He deserves a night at the movies far more than you do."

So that's how I found myself squeezed between Henry, Olive, and Jimmy Joe in the Harkin's Feed Store truck until we got to the Cameo Theatre in the village. Jimmy Joe's breath smelled of tooth powder, and his hair was slicked back. He was definitely trying to impress Olive, but for the life of me, I couldn't figure out why.

After we got our popcorn and grape sodas, I was

convinced that I would have no time alone with Henry, so the evening was a wash. "There's four seats way down in front," I said.

"You sit wherever you want. Olive and I are going to sit back here." Jimmy Joe grinned, pointing to the back row.

"Okay, that's disgusting," I said. "Henry, let's go down front."

"What's with the men's pants?" asked Henry, grinning. "Have you gone revolutionary on me?"

"They're Nancy's," I said. "She's so modern."

"And what's the deal with those two?" he asked, jerking his thumb back toward Jimmy Joe and Olive. "She looked half dead on the trip here last night, and now she's glowing."

"It's creepy beyond words. Olive's my age, and Jimmy Joe is almost twenty-three. That's illegal, for Christ's sake."

"First off, she looks at least eighteen. And it's not illegal to take someone to the movies."

"Yeah, well I'll bet whatever they're doing in the last row is illegal."

Someone shushed me because the lights had dimmed and the picture was about to start.

*

Shouting woke me in the middle of the night. At first I thought it was Da come back to haunt us, but these weren't angry shouts. They sounded more like terrified shrieks. I bolted from the sofa, almost forgetting that Sullivan had fallen asleep against my chest. Scooping him up in my arms for protection, I ran to Jimmy Joe's room, where the shouts had subsided to whimpers.

"What's the matter?" I yelled as I swung open his door, only to stop in shock at the sight before me. A sobbing Jimmy

Joe was being comforted by none other than Nancy, in the same soothing voice she used to quiet Christine yesterday.

"What are you doing in my brother's bedroom, wearing your nightshift?" I turned and almost knocked into my other brother, sending him reeling on his good leg.

"Oh, Jesus, I'm sorry." I helped Packy steady himself. "Don't go in there!"

"Stop being an arse, Jay," Packy said, pushing past me. "Nancy's a trained military nurse, for heaven's sake. She knows what she's doing."

Nancy appeared at the door. "Jay, come into the kitchen so we don't wake the baby, please. I want to explain something to you." She turned to Packy. "He's settled down for now. Go back to bed. I'll join you in a few minutes."

Nancy guided me toward the kitchen table, holding a kerosene lamp to light our way.

"Packy's promised me electricity by Christmas." She smiled.

I didn't smile back.

"I'm sorry I've upset you. I realize it must have looked very improper indeed. I apologize for not explaining everything to you yesterday."

"Explain what?" I asked, more confused than ever.

"Jimmy Joe suffers from a condition most commonly referred to as shell shock."

I took a sharp intake of breath. His hands were trembling the day he picked me up at school last March to tell me that Da had suffered a stroke.

Nancy placed her hand upon mine, reading the fear in my eyes. "It is certainly not a severe case; I saw much, much worse when I was in England and France. The work he does here on the farm has worked well as his occupational therapy, planting and working the land. This work, in addition to deep breathing exercises, calms his anxiety and reduces the tremors in his hands. He's gained such a sense of purpose and satisfaction bringing back the farm, and we'll even have indoor plumbing by spring."

"Yeah, but what about the yelling?" I asked.

"Nights are difficult for him. He has nightmares that he's being called back into service, where he saw so many of his friends suffer and die. He has terrible guilt about surviving with only his burns, while Packy lost his leg and Christie lost his life. Back in France, Jimmy Joe was awarded medals for bravery. Here, he's just another wounded veteran, wracked with nerves at the sound of sudden noises or movement. Adjusting to civilian life is difficult for him as well as most veterans after all the horror they've seen. I've nursed thousands of soldiers with this condition. There weren't enough social workers or psychologists at the Red Cross field hospitals in France. Endicott Hospital in London was better staffed. I watched and learned as much as I could."

"Does Packy have it too?" I asked, worried.

"Ironically, because of his amputation, Packy received much better care than guys like Jimmy Joe. He spent less time in action because of his injury, and spent months in hospitals, where he received round-the-clock care, including psychiatric monitoring. Jimmy Joe got a quick interview upon his discharge to check that he was fit to enter back into society. That's it."

"So Packy's scars are on the outside, while Jimmy Joe's are on the inside."

Nancy smiled. "Well stated, young lady. So now you see that I wasn't trying to seduce my brother-in-law."

I blushed.

She patted my hand. "I'm sorry. Of course you would have suspected something untoward. Jimmy Joe has these episodes quite frequently, and I'm used to calming him down. I've tried to get him to visit our clinic in the village for psychiatric counseling, but he refuses. He laughed in my face when I suggested expressing his fears through writing poetry, even though it's proven highly effective with our boys on the front who've suffered from this particular neurasthenic disorder, I mean, shell shock. And unfortunately, Mother McKenna agrees with his decision. She doesn't want me butting in."

"Ya think?" I asked, smiling. "It couldn't be more obvious that she's like a tiger protecting her cubs when you're around. Why do you call her Mother McKenna? It makes her sound like a nun in a convent."

She took both of my hands in hers and squeezed them. "I'm so grateful to have you in my corner, Jay. You and I have a lot in common, I think. And, she told me how she wishes to be addressed when Packy brought me home."

I rolled my eyes. "That's way too formal. We have to come up with a better name. You should just call her Nora, her Christian name." I apologized for jumping to conclusions, even though Nancy told me it was unnecessary. "Thank you for the trousers. I'll wash them and give them back to you tomorrow."

"Keep them," she said. "We have to shake this house up a little, my smart and modern sister-in-law."

"Thank you." I wrapped one of my many auburn curls around my finger. "How long have you had your hair bobbed?"

She touched her short mop of curls and chuckled. "Back when I was nursing in the field hospitals in France, we chopped our hair short because the tents were crawling with lice. I found it much easier to take care of, so I kept it short when I returned to the States. I wish I had a more fashion-savvy reason, but you don't worry about glamour when you're up to your knees in mud in a hospital tent."

I liked Nancy. I had to figure out a way to convince Jimmy Joe to get help for his shell shock.

*

After finally falling back to sleep on the sofa, comfortably snuggled up against my snoring Sullivan, I was awoken by voices. Now what?

I was careful to untangle myself this time so as not to disturb him. In the light of the harvest moon, I could see the bed we'd made up for Olive on the floor was empty. Oh jeez, where had she gone off to this time?

The voices were coming from outside. I could see pretty well in the moonlight, so I didn't risk waking anyone by lighting a lamp. I peered through the kitchen window. I could make out Olive and Jimmy Joe, sitting on the top step of the porch. She lit a second cigarette off the one she clamped between her teeth and passed it to him. Jimmy Joe leaned over and rested his head on her shoulder, blowing smoke circles into the night air. She ran her free hand through his hair, speaking softly. I was so confused. Lazy, moody, secretive Olive was consoling my tortured brother; he seemed to love every minute of it.

I willed myself to stay awake until Olive came back in the house and began settling herself in to sleep on the pile of quilts set on the floor. The fire in the hearth had smoldered, and the room had grown chilly.

"What are you doing with Jimmy Joe?" I whispered from my makeshift bed on the sofa.

"It doesn't concern you. Go to sleep."

"Olive, I need to talk to you about my brother. He isn't, well, what I mean is, he isn't himself since he came home from the war. Nancy's trying to help him, but he's not the type who goes in for all the newfangled therapies psychologists are coming up with to treat shell shock. Nancy said working the farm helps him. It's probably not a good idea for him to get involved with anyone right now."

"You mean it's not a good idea for him to get involved with me."

I bent my arm and leaned my chin in the palm of my hand so I could see her better in the dark. "Olive, can I speak plainly?"

"It depends on what you're about to say," she said, with a distinct tone of caution. It reminded me of Sullivan's low warning growl when someone was coming to the door. I had to tread lightly to avoid being bit.

"How did you end up falling asleep standing up in the outhouse Thursday night?"

"I was just tired, is all."

"You're always tired. You sleep through most of our classes. You sneak out most nights and start your homework at around three o'clock in the morning. Where on earth do you have to be in the middle of the night? What's going on with you?"

"I already told you, I have—"

"You have a lot going on right now. Yeah, I know. Olive, I can't figure you out. You bite anyone's head off who tries to start a conversation with you, and I feel like you're not telling me something. You're holding something back."

"Aren't we all?"

"Not like you. I mean, forgive me, but at school, pretty much everyone's afraid of you. I know I am. But tonight around Jimmy Joe, you're a different person. What's going on?"

"I've already told you that's my business, haven't I?"

Frustrated, I threw the covers off and sat up on the sofa. "Stop talking in circles, will you? I'm trying to understand, but you're making it impossible. And if you're becoming involved with my brother, who's apparently very vulnerable right now, it is my business."

Olive sat up as well and made eye contact with me in the dark. "I'd never hurt Jimmy Joe, if that's what you're worried about. We're kindred spirits, he and I, who understand each other."

"And you've figured this out since you met him at dinner a few hours ago?"

"Are you calling me a liar?"

"There you go again. Why do you always have to be so defensive and hostile? I'm not hostile toward you."

"Because you wouldn't understand where I've come from. You've been cosseted as the baby of the family and spoiled at that ridiculous school. Haviland is not the real world. Far from it."

"I have not been spoiled," I shot back, holding up my mangled fingers. "My father shut a car door on my hand while he was kidnapping my sister."

Olive paused for a minute. "Okay, I'll give you that." She paused again before continuing. "I can't tell you why I do the things I do. But when the time is right, I'll explain everything."

I sighed. "At least that's something."

"Yes, it is. It's far more than I'd say to anyone else. And you have my word, Jay. I won't hurt Jimmy Joe."

"Why is it far more than you'd say to anyone else?" I lit the kerosene lamp on the coffee table. In this light, with her hazel eyes clear and her cheeks tinged with color from the night air, Olive looked a little beautiful.

"Because you have something I want," she said, unapologetically.

"So you're only talking to me because you want me to put in a good word for you to Jimmy Joe. Is that it?" I asked, suspiciously.

"I'm not like you, Jay," she said, grabbing an ashtray from the coffee table and lighting a cigarette. "I don't need friends. I don't want to be accepted by any of those elitists at school. I couldn't care less about any of them."

"Then why did you go to the Interest Tea?" I challenged.

"Because I gave you my word," she said, tapping her ashes. "And however bad of a person I am, I don't go back on my word."

"I wouldn't have taken you for someone with principles." I smiled.

"Well, I'm full of surprises, aren't I?" She smirked.

Changing the subject, I asked, "I'm freezing. Do you want some tea?"

Olive shrugged. I took that for a yes, so I wrapped my faded daisy quilt around my shoulders and padded out into the kitchen, still wearing my black wool stockings. I let Sullivan out the kitchen door to do his business. While waiting for him to come back inside, I put the kettle on the stove and turned up the flame. Once Sullivan came in and settled himself back on the sofa, I summoned Olive to join me at the table.

"Are you going to pledge the Gilded Lilies?"

"They're never going to ask me."

"I think they have to, since your mother is an alumnus."

She sniggered. "Oh yes, my mother's an alumnus."

"What do you mean by that?" I asked, puzzled.

She ignored my question. "Why does this mean so much to you? You've got Florence and Pilar. Why do you need those toffee-nosed preps to approve of you? You're going to lose the few friends you do have if you pledge this stupid guild. You know that, don't you?"

I had to admit she had me there. "Since I started there a year ago, I've just had this fire in my belly about wanting to prove that I'm just as good as any of them." I took the kettle off the flame before it started its shrill scream. "In the village school, I never felt less than any other student. But at Haviland, it's all about who your mother was, and ruby and pearl rings, and pledging a guild. I hate having people look down at me because I live on a farm. I want to show the whole damn school that I can be a Gilded Lily the same as the next girl."

Olive nodded slowly as she stubbed out her cigarette. I watched in disbelief as she dumped teaspoon after teaspoon of Mam's carefully hoarded rainbow sugar into her tea.

"I get it, I think. I know what it's like to want to prove yourself, to feel like you're something more than a piece of garbage. But why the Gilded Lilies?" she asked.

"Because, they're—what was that you called them a few minutes ago?"

"Elitists."

"Yes, that's it." I paused to sip my tea. "They're the elitists of the school. If I can get them to accept me, everyone will, and then I won't have to prove myself anymore to anyone."

"Well, I think you're crazy, throwing away real friends for fake ones, but you seem hell-bent on doing just that."

"I'm not throwing away my real friends," I said with a little too much force.

Olive pressed her finger to her lips to shush me.

More quietly, I said, "And people are already stopping me in the hallway to ask about the Interest Tea and if I'm going to pledge. You heard what Evangeline said, once you're a Gilded Lily, you're royalty."

"Oh, and now you're taking advice from that buffoon."

I had to chuckle and give her that one. Evangeline was indeed a buffoon.

"Did you hear all the horrible things they make you go through when you're pledging?" Olive asked. "Starvation, sleep deprivation, running for miles at night? Are you sure you want to put yourself through all that just to join their dumb guild?"

I was adamant. "I mean to show them what I'm made of."

"Well, it's your funeral, I guess." Olive pumped the well at the sink, rinsed her teacup, and placed it in the dish rack to dry.

Satisfied that I had cracked the surface of this mysterious girl, I turned down the flame in the lamp and snuggled under the quilt with Sullivan. I was falling off to sleep when Olive shook my shoulder. I turned over to see what she wanted.

"If you're dead set on going through with this hare-brained pledging stunt, I'd be willing to help, if you do something for me in return."

I blinked my eyes awake in the dark. "What could you do to help me?"

"The Gilded Lilies are going to eat you alive," she began. "What is it that Florence calls you? A hayseed, that's what you are. These society girls can be malicious."

"Again, how can you help me?"

"I'm a survivor if there ever was one. I'll pledge with you and make sure you succeed. I can survive anything, as I've proven a number of times."

I thought she might be delusional at this point. "What have you survived?"

"Never mind about that. Is it a deal or isn't it?"

I hesitated. "You mentioned you wanted me to do something for you."

"Help me with Jimmy Joe," she started. "Invite me up here to your house, or invite him to school. I want to get to know him better."

"I'll think about it." I rolled back over to sleep.

*

Sullivan sneezed in my face, waking me as the sun crept over the hills to the east.

"Thanks," I said, wiping my face with the crocheted blanket I had wrapped around me on the sofa. It was then I spotted the mussed pile of quilts on the floor.

"Good Lord." I ran out to the porch, praying that Olive was having coffee there. Oh jeez, had she joined Jimmy Joe in his room after I fell asleep? Mam was gathering eggs from the chicken coop. She would have a fit if she caught Olive in Jimmy Joe's bed. My heartbeat sped up when I gently knocked on his door, careful not to wake Christine. No one came to the door. I waited a minute before walking in, dreading what I might see. The room was empty.

I turned when I heard the kitchen door open.

"What are you doing sneaking around in my room?" Jimmy Joe threw his work jacket on a wall peg.

"Where were you?" I shut his door behind me.

"Milking cows, like I do every morning. What are you up to, anyway?"

"Where's Olive?" I hissed.

"How should I know? You slept in the same room as her."

I pointed to the pile of quilts. "She's gone."

A flicker of surprise flashed in his eyes, followed by disappointment.

"I saw you out on the porch with her. Mam's going to want to know where she got off to. Olive does this all the time, you know, runs off in the middle of the night. You don't know what you're getting yourself into." I couldn't believe she had taken off after I opened up to her. I thought we were becoming friends.

"You don't know anything about her." He slammed the door behind him before heading up to the barn. Gosh, he sounded like Christie.

"What'd you say now to upset him?" Mam grabbed the percolator off the flame and filled Jimmy Joe's coffee cup. "Bring this up to him and apologize. Poor man's been working since four while you've been lounging on the sofa." She looked over my shoulder into the parlor. "And where's that girl gone off to? She's got eyes for him, that one, but he's too good for the likes of her."

I poured myself some coffee. "She, uh, had to catch the early train this morning. She ran into some kinfolk at the movies last night and promised she'd visit them down in Mount Kisco." That sounded pretty plausible.

Mam narrowed her eyes. "You're a terrible liar, Josephine. Well, good riddance to bad rubbish. Now, make yourself useful and bring your brother his coffee while it's still hot."

*

WEDNESDAY, OCTOBER 22, 1919

I awoke to a splash of cold, filthy water in my face. I opened my mouth to scream, accidently swallowing a mouthful of whatever grime I had just scraped off the tub stopper. I stood up and saluted in the corner of the lavatory, where I had fallen asleep.

"At ease, Pledge McKenna! There's no sleeping on the job." Mae threw what was left in the bucket against the wall I had just scrubbed. "Start over and get it right this time. You've got Doris's washroom to clean next, and your little nap just cost you valuable time."

I rinsed the revolting refuse out of my mouth. "What time is it?"

Mae glanced at her silver wristwatch. "Four a.m. And I'm in the mind for some ladyfingers. Produce them here, now."

Dazed from lack of sleep, I rifled through the canvas bag of treats I had spent my entire savings on to satisfy the cravings of the senior Gilded Lilies. While Mae favored ladyfingers, Doris demanded horehound drops every hour on the hour. To avoid punishment, I made sure I had enough caramels, nonpareils, licorice, and divinity to satisfy the whim of any senior who approached me. I cursed myself for being lured into this mess by the soft-spoken, dainty girl in pearls at the Interest Tea earlier in the month. It was all a charade. Mae had a vindictive streak second to no one but Doris.

"Here you are." I handed her the last of the ladyfingers I had purchased on credit from the Carmel Drug Store earlier that morning. Betty Cornish had to vouch for me to her parents, who owned the store, before they offered me a line of credit. With sugar rationing, the price of candy had skyrocketed, and I made a deal to work off my debts by sweeping up and restocking the shelves every evening. My savings continued to dwindle, mostly from satisfying the sweet tooth of every senior Gilded Lily, but also from the theft of my money, which had continued despite my changing hiding spots for my change purse. I was running on empty most days.

Mae tossed them in the bucket of bleach. "You expect me to eat these after you handled them with your disgusting hands? Are you trying to poison me? Wash your hands and give me two clean ladyfingers. Now."

"Those were the last of them." I winced, dreading what was coming.

Mae removed a book from her skirt pocket, licked the nib of her pencil, and opened to a fresh page. "You've just earned ten laps around the school grounds after dark this evening. Report to me at the tennis courts by seven thirty sharp, or you'll run twenty." She called to Olive, who had been scouring the sink. "Pledge Moody! Two ladyfingers, now."

Olive dropped her steel wool and washed her hands with soap and hot water before handing Mae two cookies from her treat bag.

"Get back to work, McKenna." Mae turned on her heels and faced Olive. "Pledge Moody, approach!"

Olive marched up to Mae and gave a stiff salute.

Mae tapped her clipboard. "The Gilded Lilies had no choice but to allow you to pledge, as your mother is an alumnus. However, Pledge Moody, we've been notified that you have been placed on academic probation due to your dismal midterm grades. We are well within our rights to strip you of your pledging pin this minute. What do you say for yourself?"

"Permission to speak, Officer Austin," I piped up from behind the sink.

"Approach, Pledge McKenna."

"I can tutor Olive to bring her up to speed," I offered, glancing sideways at my fellow pledge. I remembered how much trouble I'd gotten into last year tutoring Nathalia, but Olive had brought me this far in pledging. The Gilded Lily pledge pin I wore with pride had resulted in a rush of admiring smiles from classmates, special attention from the boys at Haviland, and cheers of good luck and well wishes from everyone all over campus. I was finally accepted as one who would soon become a member of the campus elite. And I owed it all to Olive. There was no way in hell I would have made it through the merciless hazing I'd endured over the past few weeks without her by my side. Helen, Mercy, and the others who had dropped out had been shunned by every student on campus. I wasn't going to let that happen to me.

"Very well, Pledge McKenna." Mae faced Olive. "You have one week to turn your grades around, Pledge Moody." Mae turned to leave. "One week," she repeated.

"Would it have killed you to wake me up before she came in here?" I asked Olive as I wiped the bucket clean, nauseous from imagining how much soap scum I must have ingested. Refilling it with water and bleach, I picked up the brush and started again on the wall tiles.

"I tried to, Jay, but you were out cold. I've got enough to worry about without babysitting you," she grumbled as she poured more bleach in the bucket. "The floor's never going to be clean if you don't add more bleach. What's the matter with you?"

"I can't stay awake anymore, that's what's the matter!" I leaned against the wall for a moment to rest. "Olive, tell me something. How in all that's good and holy do you manage to sleep through all your classes, yet come to life at night and put the rest of us pledges to shame? You never get tired, you outrun all of us in laps, and you plow through all these disgusting jobs like they're nothing.

How can you function for hours without food, sleep, or water?"

Olive smirked. "Trust me. This is nothing." She dipped my brush in the bleach solution and showed me how to remove the black mold in between the wall tiles.

"Well, your days of skipping classes are over, I'll tell you that." I scrubbed the tiles until they shone white. "I've got a week to get your grades up, and you are going to meet me at the library an hour before class starts every morning to study for exams. I'm not going to wake you. You've got to shape up, or they're going to toss you out."

"Who cares?" she said. "I'm only doing this to help you." She resumed sluicing the walls with bleach before scrubbing the stubborn mold.

"You'll care when I stop inviting you up to my house." I pretended not to notice her shock at my sudden assertiveness. This was war.

An hour passed, and I started to adopt that perpetually stooped stance that Mam held after a day of washing, cooking, and cleaning. My shoulders, neck, and back hurt in places I never knew existed. I was startled by an exaggerated sigh coming from the hallway.

Evangeline was at the door. At this ungodly hour, I had to admit I was glad to see a face as miserable as mine. I motioned for her to come in, but put my finger to my lips so we wouldn't get caught talking.

Her face crumbled in a sob. "I can't scrub one more toilet. I have my dignity to consider. I'm sure Mother wasn't put through this humiliation when she pledged."

In spite of my exhaustion, I smiled. "Remember how sweet Mae and Doris were when they were offering us trays of canapes? Who would ever dream they were drill sergeants in disguise?"

"Suck it up, prima donnas," Olive growled as she flushed a bucket of gray water down the toilet.

Evangeline wiped her nose with a rag from her bucket. "I was so excited when they presented me with a lily and an invitation-to-pledge card. I've wanted to be a Gilded Lily since Mother first told me about them. I can handle the silly beanies they make us wear. I can even deal with carrying around this ridiculous bag with the seniors' favorite treats. But to be woken up at midnight to scrub their privies? That's where I draw the line. I'm out." She sniffed and began blubbering. "Mother will be so disappointed." She dropped her mop and bucket on the floor. It made a loud clang as it hit the concrete. She took off her pin and handed it to me.

"You tell them, Jay. I can't face the Gilded Lilies. I'm dead to them now that I've quit. I'll be a pariah on campus. No one will want to be seen with me. My life is over." She collapsed against my shoulder in a fit of heaving sobs.

I shrugged her off of me. "Shh, Evangeline. They'll hear you. Sneak back to your room and get some sleep. Your mother will understand." I poked my head outside the door to make sure no one was in the hallway. "Go on, now."

I grabbed Evangeline's discarded mop. I hadn't been offered this luxury, and it made the work ahead easier. So this was what I was reduced to. I chuckled. I was grateful that I now had a mop head to swish around the toilet bowls, rather than my hands. My life had certainly been reduced to a sorry state of affairs.

*

I wrapped Mam's knitted muffler around my neck to ward off the chill after the sun set the following evening. I had learned over the past weeks not to overdress for these runs, as I quickly became overheated during the final laps.

Mae and Doris waited for the final lighted window to dim in the school building.

"Why do you have to wait until dark to make me start running?" I asked. "Why are these runs forbidden on campus?"

The wind blowing up from the lake had started to pick up when I walked back from sweeping up Mrs. Cornish's storefront about an hour ago. There had been no time for a dinner break. My stomach bellowed a resounding growl of protest. I ignored the looks of revulsion from my two cultured jailers.

"Never you mind about that," Doris answered, checking her slim gold wristwatch. "Worry about doing what you're supposed to do, so you won't have to run laps. Give me another horehound drop. Or better yet, leave the bag here, and I'll help myself while you're running."

Mae stomped her foot to punctuate her irritation. "I'll catch my death waiting for Pledge Ormsby in this night air. She should have been here by now to start her laps. She's accrued more demerits than any of you remaining three pledges." The heel of her T-strap shoe left an indentation in the grass. "Start running, McKenna. I'll go fetch Ormsby."

I took off in a slow jog, trying to reserve my energy for the last grueling treks up the hill that led to the dorm. I treasured a stretch of the path that gently descended down a slope to Florence and my special spot down by the stream. Tonight's solitary run freed me from the mindless Gilded Lily chatter that I was usually forced to engage in with a fellow pledge who ran off her punishment laps alongside me. Thank heaven I didn't have to listen to

Nathalia's constant bemoaning tonight. I had conveniently forgotten to tell her that we were expected at the tennis courts by seven thirty. This bought me some blessed alone time while Mae went looking for her.

I thought of Florence. Her distant courtesy had been infuriating over the past few weeks, ever since I missed the lecture. We played our roles in carrying on as normal, studying in the library, sharing meals, walking to class; but it felt forced, stilted actually. My pledging involved spending time with people we both loathed, and it drove a wedge between us that was deepening with the passage of time. Florence befriended every girl in the attic in my absence. They were a different lot altogether than the girls in the dorm who snubbed Florence and me last year. The girls from the attic did not wear the ruby and pearl rings that bedecked the hands of the third- and fourth-generation Haviland students.

Maybe the war changed people's attitudes toward things like ruby and pearl rings. Maybe the attic girls weren't randomly chosen. Maybe the girls with influence were granted rooms in Patience Hall dormitory, while the newcomers were housed in Fowler House's attic. Whatever it was, Florence attended lectures, concerts, and Saturday matinees with her friends while I was serving and cleaning up at Gilded Lily teas and mixers where I was allowed nothing to eat or drink.

On most nights, I returned to the attic well after midnight, filthy, stinking of sweat, and covered in mud and leaves from pledging out in the woods away from the scrutiny of Haviland's faculty. On some nights I didn't make it upstairs, for I was vomiting up the castor oil we pledges were forced to guzzle down as proof of our desire to belong to the Gilded Lilies.

I now found myself belonging to neither of these worlds. I was forced to be civil to the likes of Nathalia, for I couldn't make waves if I was to gain acceptance into the Gilded Lilies. In doing so, I further alienated Florence and her new friends. When I entered the attic, conversations stopped.

And why was I putting myself through this torture? Why was I denying myself simple comforts, friendship, food, and sleep? I was doing it because I was a bullheaded girl born of poor Irish immigrants with something to prove. These snot-nosed preps wanted me to fail, and I wouldn't give them the satisfaction. I was going to pass their miserable tests if it killed me. I was soon to find out how close to the truth my proclamation would ultimately prove.

I was on my tenth lap, my lungs burning with exhaustion, as I approached the dreaded hill that led up to the dining hall. The gas lamps had been snuffed an hour ago, but I knew my way in the dark by the scent of the acrid smoke still lingering in the air from Mr. Gallagher's fire burning in his metal trash can. I inhaled the musky scent of the remaining red maple leaves disintegrating into mulch. My leg muscles had long ago become rubbery, and my hunger and lack of sleep had made me dopey, as if I was wrapped in gauze. I wiped the dried spit that had gathered at the corners of my dry mouth. It had been hours since I'd had food or water. My gait had slowed, but the pain of my exertion had been replaced by an odd sideways tilt. I felt light-headed, and my vision was blurred; but it was not altogether unpleasant. Was I dying? If I was, it wasn't that bad. I was desperately thirsty, but I enjoyed this fuzzy, pain-free limbo. Maybe I could run forever. Maybe I could run all the way to Christie in heaven. I just had to keep going.

I heard the figure running behind me, but it was far too dark to see anything. My reflexes had been numbed by exhaustion. Someone knocked me over in a tangle of sharp elbows, ribs, and knees. I collapsed, my forehead soundly cracking against the first concrete step leading to the dining hall, allowing me to commence my journey toward Christie as everything crumbled around me in black.

"You stupid, foolish girl."

I wavered in and out of consciousness. I counted, one, no two, fuzzy-looking Nathalias hovering over me. My head hurt. The black was beckoning.

Long white hands, pulling me up. I fell back down.

"I just want to stay here." My words came out dripping in marshmallow sauce from Dieter's Confectionary.

She kept tugging at me. "Get up, Jay." Her voice sounded slow like the sap that ran from the maples in March. "They're trying to break you. They don't want you. Miss Chichester threatened to shut them down if they didn't choose you. You're such an idiot. Give up before they kill you."

Of course. There had to be a reason why they chose me. Now I knew.

"Thank you, Nathalia," I whispered before I surrendered to the blackness.

Chapter Six

"How long has she been out?"

I smelled that crisp, earthy scent of someone who has just come in from the cold. A kid-gloved hand touched my arm.

"Jay, it's me, Nancy. Your mother sent me. I told her I was going to be in this area making rounds. She can't get away because she's minding the baby while Eileen is working the day shift at the cigar factory. Can you open your eyes?" She sat down on the edge of my bed.

I tried to drag open my thick, heavy eyelids. The blackness gave way to a slit of blinding white. I put my hand up to shield my eyes from the sunlight coming in through the inch or so of the window not covered by the shade. The sudden movement caused my head to explode in a fireball of excruciating pain. I became sick all over Nancy. She fetched a bucket and cleaned me up.

"Lie back down and rest. I'll just sit and hold your hand if that's okay. You're in the school's infirmary with a serious concussion. Don't talk. Just try to sleep."

I tried to nod but was immediately seized by another wave of pain and nausea. I was content just feeling Nancy's hand holding mine.

*

"Take a sip of this."

I felt a teaspoon clicking against my teeth. My tongue touched something hot, but not boiling. The familiar aroma brought tears to my eyes. I swallowed a glorious sip of tea and waited for the nausea. It didn't come. I opened my eyes.

"Florence," I whispered. My throat was parched. "Can I have some more?"

"Just little sips. You don't want it all coming back up again."

I hoisted myself up to a semi-sitting position. Florence adjusted the pillow to support me.

"You're a sight for sore eyes," I said, taking the teacup from her. The tea tasted like heaven.

"You're not," she said. "You look like hell warmed over. How's that egg on your head? It's got to be four different shades of purple."

I gingerly touched my forehead. I felt a huge lump. "I fell, right?" I asked, trying to remember the night I did my laps.

"Nathalia ran into you, and then you cracked your head on the stairs that go around the back of the dining hall."

"Time's up. You'll have to leave now. Your friend needs her rest." A nurse summoned Florence to the door.

"But she just got here." I didn't want her to leave.

"I've been here for an hour. You've been snoring like a buzz saw the whole time." Florence rose and put on her Haviland coat. It still hung on her. I remembered my suspicion last year that she was probably wearing Violet's coat.

"Sorry." I reached for her hand. "Thank you for coming to visit me. It means so much that you took the time, after...after I've been acting like such an ass lately." My voice caught. I wanted to apologize for neglecting her to chase after a bunch of snobs who didn't even want me in their stupid guild, but I thought better of it. Florence deserved more than a bedside confession.

"You got that right." She adjusted her hat and left.

I sank back into the pillows to suppress the urge to vomit up the few sips of tea I had in my stomach. The room spun around me until I closed my eyes.

"You need to give your brain a chance to heal from that nasty blow you received," said the nurse, who spoke in a brogue like Mam. "Stay quiet now. No talking, no bright lights, just rest." She blocked out the offending sunlight by closing the shade until it reached the windowsill.

I nodded, fighting another wave of nausea.

I don't remember how long I was out until I heard the rustling of the curtains separating my bed from the next.

A familiar voice assured the nurse. "I'll be a minute."

"Miss Chichester." I hastily tried to smooth my hair. As always, Miss Chichester was the height of fashion in a fur-trimmed cognac velveteen suit with button trimming.

"Please don't fuss, Miss McKenna. The nurse told me not to stay long or expect you to say much. Lord have mercy, look at that bump. Are you in much pain?"

I smiled weakly. "Just when I try to move about. I can't seem to stay awake very long."

Miss Chichester nodded. "You've had a concussive brain bruise, no doubt. I've heard of such injuries. They're not to be taken lightly, I assure you. Best you stay in bed for now. No reading, no schoolwork for the time being. You're a clever girl and should have no trouble making up the work you're missing." She motioned to the stiff-backed metal chair next to my bed. "May I?"

"Of course, Miss Chichester." Imagine, my teacher asking my permission to take a seat. I would have chuckled if I could be sure I wouldn't throw up all over her embroidered scarf.

"I'm sure you're no doubt curious as to why I'm here, Miss McKenna, so I'll be brief."

She pulled a decorative hat pin from her hair, removed her large-brimmed picture hat, and laid her matching gloves across it on the nightstand next to my bed. Moistening her lips before folding her hands on her lap, she patted her well-coifed chestnut hair before continuing. "I received a visit from a Mrs. Padriac McKenna yesterday; your sister-in-law, Nancy, if I'm correctly remembering her Christian name."

"Why?" I asked, my cheeks growing a bit warm.

"You're pledging the Lily Guild, correct?" she asked, arching a groomed eyebrow.

I silently nodded, growing wary.

"Your sister-in-law is an impressive young woman. We share the same beliefs regarding the importance of women's education, suffrage, and meaningful work. Mrs. McKenna speaks highly of you. She finds you intelligent and destined for an esteemed women's college, such as my alma mater, Wellesley."

"Yes, I like Nancy as well," I whispered nervously.

"I'll not beat around the bush, Miss McKenna. As a highly trained nurse with an impeccable record serving our expeditionary forces during the war, she is suspicious of your injury."

"I don't remember discussing my accident with Nancy," I said. I barely recalled her visit at all. Was it yesterday? It might have been the day before. "I'm all mixed up with the days."

"Mrs. McKenna went to high school in Purdys with Kitty Flynn, the nurse attending you here in the school infirmary. Nurse Flynn shared with your sister-in-law the circumstances in which you were brought here. She doesn't believe the story provided by Miss Austin and Miss Nichols. Your sister-in-law shares Nurse Flynn's skepticism. As do I, Miss McKenna." She poured me a glass of water when I coughed. "As do I."

"And those circumstances relayed by Mae and Doris were what? I don't remember," I said, swallowing a tiny sip of water to quench my parched throat.

"That you stumbled upon entering Miss Austin's room. You had been summoned there to partake in afternoon tea, apparently. I have never known you to be a particularly clumsy young woman who had demonstrated any difficulty negotiating the hallways of Patience Hall. You had been nursed, overnight I might add, by Miss Austin and Miss Nichols, who are apparently accomplished caretakers who've had experience with head injuries." Her voice reached a pitch perilously close to being unsuitable for the infirmary. She composed herself by rising while replacing her hat and gloves. "I'll not take up any more of your time, Miss McKenna. You require rest. As the newly appointed advisor to a committee responsible for assuring the safety of all Haviland students, you must realize how concerned I am with regard to the grievous condition in which you were brought here. Your sister-in-law was prudent in bringing this incident to my attention."

She plumped the pillows about my head. I could smell the rosewater she had dabbed on the sides of her neck, which sent my stomach roiling again.

"We will speak again when you have been restored to robust health, Miss McKenna." Her voice had returned to a hospital-appropriate whisper. "But speak again we will. Good afternoon, Miss McKenna."

Through the open curtain, I watched Miss Chichester shake her head at Nurse Flynn, who was sterilizing thermometers.

"Kitty, that girl no more stumbled on a carpeted hallway than I rode a pony in the circus. I'll be in touch. That I can assure you."

*

"You look like you've got the weight of the world on your shoulders, miss." Nurse Flynn moved a vase of pink roses from the nightstand to a table while she cleared away a teacup and a plate of untouched toast.

"Who sent those?" I asked, trying to plait my unruly mess of hair into a fat braid.

"You've got quite the admirer. She placed her hand, palm down, above her head to approximate a height of six feet.

"A handsome lad, yea high, delivered them while you were asleep. Eyes as deep blue as the Irish sea."

"Henry," I mouthed as I sank back into my pillow, miserable that I had missed him.

"So do you feel up to telling me how you came to get that goose egg yer sporting up there on your noggin?" she asked while checking my temperature.

"I fell while pledging the Gilded Lilies," I managed while keeping the thermometer under my tongue.

"Exactly what were ye doing that caused you to fall, dearie?" she asked as she took my wrist to measure my pulse. She wore the same skeptical look as Mam when she was trying to get the truth out of me.

"I tripped when I was running," I answered vaguely.

"Running down the hallway of the dorm?" she asked as she wrote my vital signs down on her clipboard.

"Yes, ma'am," I whispered.

"That's your story and you're sticking to it, eh?" she answered in a clipped voice. She filled my glass with water from a fresh pitcher.

I nodded dumbly, wishing I could disappear beneath the scratchy wool blanket she tucked in around me.

"Well, I think your story's a load of malarkey, Miss McKenna, and you're doing yourself no favors covering up for those hoity-toity Gilded Lilies, but that's just my opinion." She cleaned my face with a soft cloth dipped in warm, soapy water from a small basin.

Tears gathered in my eyes from her resemblance to Mam, washing me like a child with her rough, weathered hands.

"I can't let them break me. They win that way." I swallowed hard, inhaling Nurse Flynn's scent of rubbing alcohol, carbolic soap, and starched cotton. "They were forced by Miss Chichester to let me pledge. Nathalia told me the night I fell."

"For the love of Saint Jude, child, you're not thinking of going on with this stupidity? You can't be that daft, are ye? They as good as left you for dead, waiting all night before bringing you here."

"You don't know how hard it is to feel that you'll never be accepted, that you'll never fit in," I protested.

To my horror, Nurse Flynn busted out laughing. "Oh, that's a good one. I like that." She wiped tears of laughter from her eyes and put her hands on her hips. "I don't know what it's like not to fit in? Me, a tenant farmer's daughter from County Sligo? Child, I arrived here the same way yer mammy and da did, with nothing more than the clothes on me back."

"But you've got a job as a nurse in a respectable school," I protested. "You don't know what it's like to have to claw your way through classes where nobody accepts you."

She stopped laughing. "You have a lovely friend, a colored girl, whom I'm certain hasn't had an easy time fitting in at Haviland, who sat with you for over an hour here today while you slept. She's a true friend. There has not been one Gilded Lily who darkened the door in this infirmary since they brought you in three days ago. And you are so very wrong, about my 'getting a job' at this school. I've had more doors slammed in my face than you could ever imagine. I've had to score the highest in my class on nursing examinations, ignore the 'No Dogs or Irish Need Apply' signs on hospitals and doctors' offices, and listen to the 'Shanty Irish' and 'Potato Farmer' insults since I stepped off the boat that brought me here. I'm made of stronger stuff than you are, miss, and if you don't get over that 'Poor me' complex when you don't get your way, you're going nowhere."

*

By the fifth day in the infirmary, I was bored to tears. Nurse Flynn had strict rules. To heal my brain, she banned me from reading, writing letters, doing homework, or turning on the bedside lamp. Olive had stopped by the previous day while I was sleeping. She had left some of her completed assignments for me to check, but Nurse Flynn forbade me from even glancing them over for errors. I was impressed with Olive's effort, but worried that I was at risk for falling behind while I was cooped up in this sterile prison. While I lived for visitors, I was prohibited from holding a conversation for more than ten minutes because Nurse Flynn didn't want to tire me out. Basically I either slept or lay awake in the darkened cubicle all day. Therefore, I was beyond thrilled to hear the voice of my dear mentor as she burst in through the door of the infirmary.

"Mein God! What have you done to my poor, sweet Jay? The secretary in the main office said she wasn't in class, and they sent me down the road to some filthy, dilapidated shack overrun with cats." Ruth Lefkowitz swept into the room, swathed in a black seal-silk wrap coat with a raccoon fur collar. On her head rested a matching velvet hat with an upturned front brim. She rushed to my bed and enveloped me in a tight embrace.

"Watch her ribs!" Nurse Flynn cautioned.

"Jay, does your mother know the squalor you are forced to live in?" asked Ruth.

"She told me we are in no position to complain because Florence is footing the bill for my room and board. Plus, Florence is staying with me. I'm fine."

Ruth swept her hand in front of me. "Apparently you are not. I want you in school benefiting from the education I paid for. The nurse said you were running in the dark and someone knocked you down. Who were you running from?"

I explained about pledging for the Gilded Lilies and how I had to run laps to work off my demerits.

Ruth huffed her exasperation and loosened the cashmere scarf from around her neck. "Why on earth are you wasting your time with this foolishness when you should be studying? Surely your summer in Albany has taught you that you are made for better things than the Gilded Lilies, for goodness sake."

I stuck my chin out. "Because they don't want me in their precious guild. I want to prove to them I can survive any test they put me through."

Again that sweep of the hand. "Clearly you cannot, from the look of things. Stop this nonsense at once, Jay. I need you healthy to head up an undercover mission to expose a sleazy, underhanded manager who is moving to a factory recently opened in your hometown of Brewster. There's been a list of complaints sent to my department in Albany, and you are just the person I need to nail this creep to the wall."

Excited, I propped myself up against my pillows. "When can I start?"

Nurse Flynn popped her head through the curtain. "I'm sorry, Miss Lefkowitz. We mustn't tire Miss McKenna out if we want her to return to classes tomorrow."

"No, I'm fine. Really. I want to hear more from Ruth about this mission."

Ruth leaned over and kissed me on the forehead. "I'll speak to Nurse Flynn about when it will be safe for you to travel. I'll send you a telegram to let you know when to take the train to meet me in the city. There's people I want you to meet. Get some rest now so you'll be ready for your first mission."

"Undercover mission? Exposing underhanded managers?" Nurse Flynn came into my cubicle to collect an empty teacup. "Miss McKenna, do you work for the government?"

"That she does, Nurse Flynn. That she does," said Ruth as she was leaving. "Get well, Jay."

*

FRIDAY, OCTOBER 31, 1919

My first week back to school was a tug-of-war between trying to catch up on five days of missed lessons and homework assignments and resting my eyes to keep the nausea at bay. This proved nearly impossible, as reading sent my eyes into a tailspin, and the bright lights of the classroom sent me to the lavatory to vomit the last meal I was able to get down. Somehow, I managed to catch up on my work, and I slowly started to feel like myself again. Thank God I was recovering, because I had resumed my early morning tutoring sessions with Olive, so my days were never-ending.

Halloween night found Nathalia, Olive, and me, the last three remaining pledges, lined up along the dark shores of Lake Gleneida. While Florence and the others were dressing up for the school costume contest, I had to turn down Henry's invitation to the Monster Halloween Dance at the Brewster Fire Department to be here. The clocks had been turned back on October 26, so even though it was barely past five o'clock, the sky was already dark. Later on, I realized this was probably deliberate so no one could witness what went on.

"Tonight, ladies, is your final test. Whoever survives this feat of stamina and strength will become the next Gilded Lily. Well, get in." Mae pushed us toward the lake's edge.

"What do you mean, get in?" asked Olive.

Mae pointed to the black water on this moonless night. "In the drink, the three of you. We'll meet you on the shore by Smalley's."

Nathalia backed away. "No, no, no. I almost drowned in this lake. I can't go back in. You can't make me. I'll die. Tell them, Jay. Tell them what happened."

"Nathalia stole my friend's car at the Valentine's Day Dance and ridiculed my boyfriend until he let her crash it through the ice on this lake. My friends and I pulled Nathalia out of the water. My friend's car is somewhere at the bottom. Does that about sum it up, Nathalia?"

"Yes, I heard about that," said Doris. She turned to Nathalia. "Too bad. Swim to the other side or you're out."

Nathalia shook her head and started weeping. "You can't do this to me. I've worked myself to the bone. My mother was a Gilded Lily. She'll be furious at you for torturing me like this. I can't do it. I tell you I can't!" She was sobbing hard now into a lace-edged handkerchief.

Doris came to the water's edge once more. "One down, two to go. Which one of you will emerge from the lake as a Gilded Lily? Get in the water, now. The wind's picking up, and I'm getting cold. I have to head over to the other side."

"Oh, well we wouldn't want you to get cold now, would we?" I snapped. I started undressing.

"What in the name of Mike are you doing?" asked Mae. "Put your clothes back on this instant."

"Nope." I stripped down to my white cotton vest and drawers. "As I said, I've done this before. I'm not having my clothes weigh me down. My clothes and shoes better be waiting for me when I reach the shore by Smalley's, or you'll be paying for a new uniform." I started wading into the water, my feet sinking into the muddy bottom. It was cold, but not freezing like last February. "Come in, Olive, it's not that bad. Let's show these snobs they can't break us."

Olive plunged in, fully clothed.

"Pledge McKenna's lost her mind," Doris called to Mae. "Coming off a concussion, and she wants more." She called to me in the water. "It's your funeral, Jay. Drown if you have a mind to. See you on the other side." The two of them pointed and laughed at me swimming in my underwear.

I turned back to Olive, who was standing about chest-deep in water. "Come on, Olive, we'll swim together." I started treading water to save energy for later on in the swim.

"I can't," she said.

"Sure you can. We'll help each other."

"I can't swim." She turned around and started walking toward the shore.

"Well, that's your misfortune," said Doris. "You're out. Grab your things and go home."

I wasn't prepared to do this alone. "Can't she use a life jacket? I can grab one out of one of the fishing boats on the shore. Come on, Doris. She's come this far. Can't you give her a chance?"

"Nope," called Mae. "That'd be cheating. You're out, Moody."

Olive looked at Mae with venom in her eyes. She trudged out of the water, came nose to nose with Doris and Mae, and told them in no uncertain terms exactly where they could shove their Lily Guild.

And then I was alone in the water. The skin on my legs was numb to my touch under the water, which was growing colder. I felt lake trout nipping at my ankles but brushed it off as my imagination. I began to paddle slowly after the rest treading water. There was the dimmest of light emerging from a window in the courthouse across the lake. I willed my limbs to propel me toward the light, imagining it was from a lamp on the desk of some over-worked law clerk.

The Gilded Lilies didn't know who they were up against this time. I had pulled two people from a submerged car when this water was twice as cold. My resolve to swim across the lake grew stronger with every stroke. At times, swimming seemed effortless, as if the overworked law clerk was pulling me toward his light on the faraway shore. Strength flooded my body. I kept repeating, "They're not going to break me."

When my headache returned, I took my time, resting on my back. When my leg muscles began to cramp, I shook them out. When the nausea came, I gave in to it, retching bile. No one could see me.

Midway across the lake, the wind picked up, sending ripples across the black surface. I swallowed a mouthful of water and started choking. *It's not as bad as the filthy slop from the bucket I swallowed when Mae threw it at me,* I reasoned. Despite the fishy smell, I knew the lake water was relatively clean. I relaxed my throat muscles and summoned more stamina. I was halfway done.

I heard my name being called from the shore. I had to conserve energy. I wouldn't waste my breath reassuring the likes of Mae and Doris that I was still alive. Let them think I'd drowned. That would serve them right.

The water must have lowered my body temperature, be-cause I couldn't stop my teeth from chattering. My eyelids were growing heavy. My tired, concussive brain was trying to convince me that if I could just float on my back and sleep, just for a little while, I would regain some strength.

No! my body screamed. *You have to fight against sleep. Don't give in. Keep going.* I flipped over from my back to my stomach and lifted my arm over my head, scooping the water in huge handfuls. Every movement was painful. My legs were seized by cramps. My fingers were puckered. Another gulp of water, more retching, more sleepiness. I closed my eyes to rest them and pumped steadily in the dark. I lost all sensation of time, concentrating on keeping my lungs filled with precious oxygen. Inhale, exhale, repeat. Nothing else mattered. I just needed to breathe. As I drew closer to the shore, I didn't even try to move much. The wind had shifted to my back, propelling me toward the light.

Panicked voices shouted my name, coming from the light. I could make out the columns and stone steps of the courthouse. Just a few more strokes would get me to the shore. I heard a splash. Someone was coming toward me.

"Take my hand," cried Doris. "I'll pull you in."

I pushed her hand away and staggered out of the water. My legs buckled under me, and I collapsed on the hard, frosted shore, vomiting lake water.

"Is she dead?" Mae sobbed. "Please let her not be dead!"

"She's practically naked!" Someone covered me with my Haviland cardigan.

I clung to the wool, absorbing its warmth.

"We've got to get her out of here before someone calls Officer Belden. Everybody's out celebrating Halloween, and we're bound to get noticed!"

I struggled to get up but fell back. I stayed on my hands and knees for a few minutes, trying to regulate my breathing. I heard the worried chatter of other Gilded Lilies gathering around me. Finally, I forced my cramped legs to support my body.

"Give me my clothes."

Mae produced my uniform, stockings, and shoes. Hiding behind a tree, I hid my wet underthings under a boat and got dressed. If I wasn't freezing to death, I would have chuckled thinking about the poor fisherman who would find my vest and drawers the next morning when he came to the lake for a quiet morning of fishing.

When I came back fully dressed, Mae smiled warmly. "Won't you come back to my room so we can celebrate? We have an announcement to make. Doris?"

Taking both of my numb hands in hers, Doris began. "We have something to tell you. We've reached a unanimous decision. No one has ever swum across Lake Gleneida before. You gave us quite a scare when we didn't hear from you."

Mae nudged her. "Tell her, Doris. My feet are cold."

"Yes, do tell," echoed the others, shivering against the chilly wind blowing off the lake.

"On behalf of the Gilded Lilies, I'd like to officially welcome you as our newest member. Congratulations." She clasped my still-freezing hands. All the other Lilies peppered my blue cheeks with air kisses.

I backed away, remembering Olive's parting words. "You can shove your Lily Guild where the sun doesn't shine."

*

"For the love of Mike, what happened to you?" cried Florence, or I think it was Florence. She was dressed as a harlequin, wearing a black mask over her eyes. "You look like a drowned cat!"

Louise, or rather Little Bo Peep, ran over and relieved me of my cardigan after placing her shepherd's hook on the floor. "She's freezing to death! Let's get her over to the fireplace to warm her up. Someone put the kettle on."

I stifled a laugh when she bent over, exposing her eyelet-edged pantalettes.

"You stink like fish," said Pilar, alias Joan of Arc, in full armor and a sword. Clanking, she wrapped me in a crocheted blanket that smelled of cat pee, rubbing warmth back into my goose-pimpled arms.

"Holy smoke! You did it, didn't you? You crazy girl, you've gone and swam the length of Lake Gleneida, haven't you?" Olive uncharacteristically descended the stairs from the attic to join us in the parlor. Even though she was not in costume, she resembled Moses parting the sea, as every girl, in fear and trepidation, cleared a wide path for her.

"Is what she's saying true, Jay? Did you actually swim across the whole lake in the dark?" asked Pilar.

"I...I guess that's exactly what I did." It didn't seem believable, now that it was all said and done.

"Should I fetch Doc Birdsall? The poor child must have hypothermia." Miss Hazel flittered around the room like a fussy hen, flapping her short arms to and fro.

"Calm yourself, sister," scolded Miss Tillie. She came to me and pressed the back of her hand to my forehead. She smiled, revealing buck teeth. "She must be made of hearty stock. Take a look. The color's already coming back to her cheeks. Let her sit a spell in front of the fire and drink some strong, hot tea. She'll be fit as a fiddle in no time."

Miss Hazel clattered about the kitchen, nervously preparing a tea tray while I recalled my lake adventure.

"Maybe the overworked law clerk is your true love, and he shone his beacon in the courthouse to lead you to his heart." I thought Pilar was going to swoon as she spun a confection of romantic possibilities.

At this point I looked up and observed that Will had come out of his bedroom and had assumed his typical stance of leaning against the wall, arms crossed, watching Florence.

"So this means you're a Gilded Lily, I assume, given that Olive can't swim and Nathalia was too traumatized to go in the water," Florence said drily.

"Mae and Doris announced that I was a Gilded Lily, yes," I answered, sipping the glorious amber nectar swirled with sweet cream that Miss Hazel had placed lovingly in my chilled hands.

"And so you graciously accepted," Florence pressed.

"Actually, I repeated what Olive so poetically expressed when they told her to leave." I felt the tea warming every blood vessel in my body.

Olive shook her head, grinning. "No way. You couldn't have."

"I most certainly did." I stood up on my still-shaky legs so everyone in the room could hear me. "I told them exactly where they could shove their Lily Guild."

A moment of stunned silence descended on the group, followed by the hoarsest, roughest, chain-smoking laugh I had ever heard in my life. Olive Moody was choking with laughter, wheezing and coughing like an old man. Pilar's giggling followed, which in turn set off Florence collapsing into whoops of laughter so hard tears started rolling down her face. At this point everyone in the room was doubled over in hysterics. Everyone but one, that is.

"I will not tolerate vulgarity in this house! This is a house of—"

"All right, all right, Miss Tillie, keep your shirt on," said Olive, calming down at last. "The girl just swam clear across the lake. Give her a break, will ya?"

"I say this calls for a celebration," announced Miss Hazel. "Sister, might such an auspicious occasion as this call for a bit of something from Father's still?"

"Well, I don't know. The fool girl did swim at least a mile in the dark. I did squirrel some away for an 'auspicious occasion' as you have so eloquently coined this rather rare phenomenon. Let me get some down at my shed."

"Of course Miss Tillie would 'squirrel' some away down at her house of horrors taxidermy shed. How appropriate," said Florence. And then she sat next to me. "I'm so proud of you for turning them down, Jay. I know you feel you had something to prove, and you nearly got yourself killed—twice, I might add—but I hope you finally realize that you are better than all that nonsense, once and for all."

I nodded. "I think I'm good now. I don't have any burning desire to scrub Mae's toilet, get my skull bashed by Nathalia, or jump in the lake outside of swimming season ever again."

Miss Tillie returned with a dusty brown jug stuck with a cork. Miss Hazel emptied the cupboards of every available jelly glass, and we toasted my feat of stamina and strength with a drop each of the potent product from Father Fowler's still.

Will brought two glasses over to Florence and handed her one. She laughed and clinked her glass to his. "Bottoms up!" she said as they both downed their shots.

Covered in cats pawing and kneading my lap, my shoulders, and my feet, I downed the whiskey and felt warmth return to my body at last.

"Hope you can get that still up and running by January, Miss Tillie. The country's going dry, and you'll have a lot of thirsty people willing to pay good money for whatever you can cook up in your daddy's still," announced Olive with a hiccup.

Miss Tillie's and Miss Hazel's eyes lit up with dollar signs.

Chapter Seven

I nodded off a few times during morning vespers, dreaming about the luxurious bath I was allowed to soak in after my night swim. After two shots of their father's moonshine, Miss Hazel and Miss Tillie temporarily lifted the ban on more than three inches of tepid water. I filled the bathtub to the tippity top with scalding, albeit rusty-brown, water and poured in whatever was left in an old box of Epsom salts I found stored behind the skirt that hid the pipes under the sink. I stayed there until every cell of my body was warm. I dressed in my heaviest flannel nightgown and piled on every blanket and quilt I had brought with me. I slept like a baby and awoke only when my alarm rang for the dreaded vespers.

Motion outside the parlor window caught my attention, and I straightened up. The Western Union telegraph messenger was turning into the Fowlers' yard. He rapped on the door, interrupting Miss Tillie's reading of the scripture. Annoyed, she motioned for me to answer the door, as I was the closest.

The messenger didn't look any older than I was but was dressed in a sharp blue uniform complete with a matching cap. He reached across a leather strap that crossed his chest to retrieve a telegram from his bag. "You Miss Josephine McKenna?" he asked, squinting in the early morning sun.

"Yes," I answered, excited as he handed me the official-looking paper. The messenger tipped his cap to me and rode off.

Vespers had by this point disintegrated into a hoard of girls hovering by the door, wondering who on earth would send me a telegram. Though ignored, Miss Tillie kept reading from her Bible.

Miss Hazel clasped her pudgy hands together in expectation as Baxter the squirrel, clad in a crocheted jacket, perched upon her shoulder. "Don't keep us in suspense, Miss McKenna!"

"Yes, tear it open and read it aloud," said Florence.

"Okay, let's see." I gently removed the telegram from its envelope and started reading the encrypted message. "Received at Carmel NY Nov 1. Then there's a bunch of numbers and letters followed by the word *Paid*. Via Carmel. Josephine McKenna. Seminary Hill Road. Jay STOP Take nine o'clock a.m. train to Grand Central Saturday November 1 STOP Will meet you there STOP Ruth Lefkowitz."

"Ruth is going to meet a train that's leaving the Carmel Station in fifteen minutes, Jay!" shouted Florence. "Grab your purse, hat, and coat, and hightail it to the depot as fast as those tired legs can carry you."

"After last night, it should be a cinch," said Olive as she groggily made her way down the stairs.

"You missed morning vespers, Miss Moody," said Miss Tillie.

"I'm sure you put in a good word for me with the man upstairs," she said, yawning and stretching as she lifted the percolator off the gas ring and poured a cup. "Coffee, Miss Tillie?" She smiled as she offered the cup to Miss Tillie.

Miss Tillie held her hand up to her forehead. "Don't mind if I do. My head is feeling rather poorly this morning."

Olive nodded and grinned, stirring at least three teaspoons of precious sugar in her coffee.

*

My legs burned as I ran to the Carmel train depot. I was unfamiliar with this station, so I initially panicked when I saw the black cowcatcher nosing away from the station, with its wheels and axles starting to turn, a plume of black smoke rising up into the gray November sky. I picked up my pace and yelled for the train to stop.

"Is that you, Jay?" called a conductor, hanging out one of the doors on the second car of the train.

"Chester, yes, it's me! I've got to be on this train!" I screamed above the screeching sounds of the train's groaning engines.

"Gimme your hand and I'll pull you up," Chester called, lowering his beefy, freckled hand to me.

Holding my hat on my head with one hand, I threw my valise through the open door, grabbed Chester's outstretched hand with my other, and felt myself being hoisted up into the air onto the stairs of the train.

"Thank you so much." I bent over a bit to try to catch my breath.

"What are you doing in this neck of the woods, Jay?"

"I go to school at Haviland, and I received a telegram to take this train to Grand Central."

"Well aren't you all grown up going to a fancy school and traveling to the city by yourself. Jimmy Joe never mentioned anything about his baby sister turning into a proper young lady."

"No, he wouldn't." I grinned and let Jimmy Joe's old boss escort me to an empty seat on the crowded train, which was surprising for a Saturday morning.

Chester punched a ticket and stuck it behind my seat.

"What do I owe you?" I fished around in my purse for some change.

"Your money's no good here, kid. Family discount." Chester tipped his conductor hat and moved on to collect fares from the passengers behind me.

Exhausted from the previous night's exertions, I was lulled to sleep by the steady motion of the train. It wasn't until Chester shook my shoulder that I woke up, wiping drool from my coat collar.

Luckily, Chester mustn't have noticed my drooling, because he had already passed my seat, cupping his mouth with one hand as he shouted, "Grand Central Station will be our final stop! Next stop, Grand Central! Check your seat for your belongings before disembarking the train, please."

I grabbed my purse and valise, adjusted my hat, and followed the line of passengers walking unsteadily down the aisle waiting to exit the train. I had to grip the back of each seat to steady myself against the swaying car.

The long tunnels of Grand Central pitched the train into darkness. When it was time to get out, a wall of stifling heat and dirty coal smoke slapped me in the face. I lost myself in the mass exodus of people emerging from trains and just followed the crowd until we reached doors that opened into a grand terminal, complete with massive train timetables. I stopped and glanced up to study the zodiac mural painted on the ceiling. Against a soft aqua sky, the constellations of Orion and Pegasus had stars that actually twinkled. Ahead of me was the famous gold clock atop the circular information kiosk. I'd never seen so many people rushing about in my entire life. To my right, passengers lined up in front of windows where tellers issued tickets to all points north and east. Newsboys shouted the day's headlines, and men sat on elevated chairs, having their shoes polished. How on earth was I ever going to find Ruth in this throng of humanity?

The crowd pushed me along to an exit marked Forty-Second Street. I had little choice but to make my way to the doors and squeeze through like everyone else. Once outside, I was treated to the cacophony of honking automobile horns, police whistles, and the clang of trolley car bells I remembered from my time here over our last Christmas break. People were battling to get into a line of taxicabs parked along the curb. A crowd was gathered around a car parked a bit further down Forty-Second Street. I suddenly heard my name being called.

"Over here, Jay!" The crowd of newspaper reporters parted enough to let the man in his signature brown derby summon me to a shiny black Model T. Governor Alfred E. Smith took his stogie from between his lips. "Sorry, folks, I've been sent to escort this young lady to the Henry Street Settlement House."

He took my elbow. "Jay! So nice to see my scrappy little friend again. Ruth's waiting in the car."

He called to the relentless reporters scrambling for a story. "I'll see you in the funny papers."

"C'mon, Governor, just one quote on your connection with Tammany Hall," barked a bespectacled cub reporter whose loud plaid suit wore him. He noticed me on Al's arm.

"Why hello there, sweet thing." The cub reporter attempted to introduce himself to me.

"Scram!" Al pushed away the reporter, firmly took my elbow, and ducked me into the opened back door of the Model T.

"Thank goodness you found us," said Ruth from behind the wheel. I sank into the plush back seat, which was upholstered in seamed black leather.

"I'm sorry I couldn't come inside to meet you, but I didn't want to give up this good parking spot." She jerked her thumb behind her. "These cabs have been honking at me to move for the past half hour, but the reporters wouldn't let Al pass to fetch you from your train."

She called out the window, "Vultures, that's what you are!" before pressing down on a button on the floor of the car with the heel of her boot and pulling out into traffic.

"Hey, kid, Ruth here tells me you got yourself into a bit of a jam with those society girls at your school," called Al from the passenger seat. "You don't need those highbrows. I had to quit school in the seventh grade after my pa died. I learned everything I needed to know scaling fish at the Fulton Fish Market. Those windbags up in Albany don't know what to make of me, which is just the way I like it. Why don't you just come up and work for Ruth and me now?"

Ruth clipped Al on his ear. "She needs an education. I keep telling you, girls need to do more than work in a fish market if they want to become governor of New York someday." She turned back to me once we were stuck in traffic. "Let me look at you. I see your color has returned to your cheeks. How are you feeling?"

"I'm well, thank you." I figured I'd leave the tale of the

previous night for later on. I ran my fingers along the seams of my luxurious seat. "When did you get a new car?"

Ruth patted the steering wheel. "The car salesman at the Ford dealership said that this year's Model T was built to withstand all types of weather. I asked him if it would survive crashing into a frozen lake." She chuckled when I cringed, remembering Nathalia driving Ruth's white roadster into Lake Gleneida.

"You must be famished after the long train ride," said Al. "We'll stop at Katz's delicatessen. I want to bring sandwiches to Lillian."

"Who are you fooling?" Ruth laughed. "You want Katz's corned beef for yourself."

"You got me there, Ruth," Al said as he puffed smoke rings like Pilar.

"Won't Katz's be closed for the Sabbath? Today's Saturday, right?" I asked.

"Very good, Jay," Ruth remarked. "Sadly, Jewish laborers have to work on Saturday, because the factories observe the Christian Sabbath of Sunday, so their wives shop on Saturday and serve the main meal of the week on Sunday when their husbands are home to enjoy it."

We pulled up to the curb on the corner of Ludlow and Houston Street. Many of the storefronts had Hebrew writing on them.

Grabbing her large wicker shopping basket, Ruth stepped up onto the sidewalk. Upon entering the packed deli, Ruth elbowed her way through a crowd of women speaking what sounded like a combination of Russian, German, and Polish. Al and I followed. We reached a glass case displaying trays of pickled herring and chopped liver alongside pots of steaming matzoh ball soup and deep purple borscht. Speaking in Yiddish, she ordered and

filled her basket with fried potato knishes, half sour pick-
les, corned beef sandwiches, individual tin cups of egg
custards, and bottles of cream soda. Upon recognizing Al,
the crowd broke into a spontaneous, heavily accented ren-
dition of "East Side, West Side," Al's campaign song.

"Does this mean I can count on your vote when I run
for re-election?" Al joked with the crowd.

We managed to maneuver both the heaping basket
and ourselves through the bustling crowd back out to the
automobile.

"Want to give her a whirl, Jay?" Ruth asked, handing
me the key to the car. "Al doesn't drive, and I hate Lower
East Side traffic."

"You bet I do!" I took the keys and jumped into the
driver's seat.

Once she deposited Al and her grocery basket in the
back seat, Ruth leaned over and pointed out the neutral,
reverse, and brake foot pedals, where to insert the key on
the dashboard, and the button on the floor I would need
to press to the start the car. The accelerator and distrib-
utor were on the underside of the steering wheel. The
choke was next to the speedometer on the dashboard.
There was also a tall brake handle coming up from the
floor of the car that I would have to pull back to stop the
car.

"I'll let you know when to turn onto Henry Street," Ruth
said as I pulled the Model T out into the traffic of delivery
wagons, dray horses pulling carts piled high with barrels
of beer, telegraph messengers on bicycles, push carts, and
vendors hawking their wares. Other drivers leaned on
their horns, shouting and waving their arms to no avail. I
enjoyed every minute of snaking the car through throngs
of people arguing over the price of vegetables, getting

their knives sharpened, and yelling at the raggedy street urchins playing in the street.

After we turned onto Henry Street, I pulled up alongside a line of redbrick buildings. Children called to each other on a playground. Once inside, Al gave our names to the receptionist and stated that Miss Wald was expecting us. We were ushered down a hallway lined with classrooms. In one, adult students sat at canvases, while a short-tempered instructor criticized their paintings. In the next classroom, a lively woman pointed to words scratched across a blackboard.

"Repeat after me. How are you? I am fine, thank you."

Adults and teens alike repeated the words with heavy accents from around the globe. Near the end of the hall, a nurse instructed mothers with infants on proper hygiene and nutrition for newborns. From beyond two closed doors, I heard a piano and a chorus singing tunes from *The Pirates of Penzance.*

At the end of the hallway, we approached a dark wood door bearing the name *Lillian Wald, Founder* stenciled in gold. Ruth turned to me, put down her basket, and rested her hands on my shoulders.

"The woman you are about to meet is sure to have a profound impact on your future career as a social worker. As the word on the door states, Lillian started the Henry Street Settlement House. You've just seen for yourself all the people who are benefiting from her hard work. She is also an advocate for children's, labor, immigrant, civil, and women's rights. She has professional contacts all over the world. Lillian Wald is the woman you want to impress with your passion for the same people she is interested in helping. I advise you to take notes and ask questions. Opportunity is knocking, Jay, and now is the time to answer."

"Ruth, you're scaring the poor kid!" scolded Al.

"Thanks for not putting any pressure on me." I grinned. "My knees are knocking together now, for heaven's sake!"

Al introduced himself to the fashionably slim secretary, Miss DeLuca, who calmly checked her appointment schedule, took our coats, and directed us to take a seat in her office. She wore her navy silk poplin dress with mandarin sleeves of Georgette crepe like a fashion model. The buttons running down the panel front were shaped like pearls.

Miss DeLuca announced our arrival and led us in to Miss Wald's office.

"Al, Ruth, what an honor!" A woman I judged to be about ten years older than Ruth removed her bifocals and came out from behind a pile of correspondence on her desk to greet us. "And please introduce me to your protégé."

Al presented me to Miss Wald. "You couldn't have a better person to catch this thug, Tassone," he said while resting his stogie in an ashtray. "How's Florence?" he asked as he mussed the top of my hair after I took my school beret off.

"Who's this Tassone?" I asked.

"We'll get to all of that soon enough," he said as he eyed Ruth's grocery basket. "I'm starved." He unwrapped a hot knish wrapped in butcher paper and inhaled its tantalizing aroma. "Come on, kid. Let's feast before we get down to business."

"You know my weakness, Ruth." Miss Wald smiled as she bit into her corned beef on rye. She was about Ruth's height, with pleasant, deep brown eyes hooded with slightly heavy lids. Fine lines were vertically etched in the space between her well-groomed brows, and she wore a high-crown fur hat. Her wool poplin belted suit had two columns of buttons running down the back of the coat.

Al patted his stomach after he finished his sandwich and cream soda. "Ruth, you spoil me. I don't deserve you as my advisor."

"I know," she said, handing him his egg custard.

I had to remind myself that Al had a wife and Ruth enjoyed her freedom as a single woman, because the two of them conversed like an old married couple.

Ruth nodded to the impressive pile of letters sitting in Miss Wald's "In" box. "I see your expertise remains in high demand."

Miss Wald handed Ruth and me a letter inviting her to speak about public health nursing at the upcoming Westchester Red Cross Conference. "I simply have to find time to speak on a topic so close to my heart." She flipped the pages of her desk calendar to May. "It'll be a tight May 13, but I will not sleep soundly if I don't attend."

"My sister-in-law was a nurse for the Red Cross over in France and England during the war," I piped up, hoping I sounded more intelligent than I felt. "She's a visiting nurse with Florence Shove's District Nursing Association of the town of Southeast, where we live."

"Miss Shove provides an invaluable service for your rural community. She has asked for my assistance in persuading your board of education to pay for a school nurse. Please tell your sister-in-law to assure Miss Shove that I will not relent on this matter until Brewster school children enjoy the benefit of a full-time nurse in their buildings."

"Lillian began her career as a nurse," Ruth informed me, "and she's credited with leading the crusade to establish public health nursing as well as public school nursing."

Now I felt like a moron, because I basically proved to Miss Wald that I was ignorant of the role she played in enabling Nancy to work as a visiting nurse. I shut my mouth until I could regroup. After an adequate period of silence on my part while Al, Ruth, and Miss Wald chatted about progress toward gaining federal suffrage for women, I tried again.

"Forgive me, but my curiosity is getting the best of me. Where do I fit in to all of this?"

"I told you this one is up for working undercover for the benefit of our joint interests, Miss Wald," said Al, lighting up another cigar. "She's inquisitive and eager to get started."

"Exactly." Ruth nodded and handed Miss Wald an envelope she had stashed in her large crocodile purse.

"Wow." She let out a long whistle as she lowered her glasses on her nose and read Ruth's report under the light of her desk lamp. "Quite a rap sheet."

"Yes," said Al, rifling through a stack of papers from his briefcase. "Complaints to labor boards across the northern Bronx and Westchester. Failing grades on fair labor practice reports, safe work environment standards inspection reports. Unacceptably high employee incident and injury reports, failed air quality reports, high employee turnover rates, and far too many formal complaints of inappropriate behavior and harassment charges."

Al handed the reports over for my perusal. "Take a look at what you're getting yourself into, kid." Turning his attention back to Miss Wald, he said, "I want to nail this creep to the wall, the sooner, the better. Who the heck does he think he is, ignoring the fair labor laws I've worked for years to get passed?" I knew when his cigar flicked up and down between his teeth that he was angry.

"How has he managed to stay employed this long?" asked Miss Wald, thumbing through Ruth and Al's paperwork.

Ruth raised her eyebrows. "Remember that saying about how you can't shoot a moving target? Well, it applies to criminals as well. This sleazebag has moved from city to city, town to town, from Pelham Bay up to Carmel, always following a failed inspection or a filed complaint. I detected a pattern, see?"

She unfolded and spread a chart across Miss Wald's desk, pointing to dates, locations, and incident reports. "A complaint was filed in August of 1917 regarding inadequate lighting in a Mount Vernon tool and die factory where Larry Tassone, our perpetrator, was serving as manager. The next failed health and hygiene report filed in February 1918 has Mr. Tassone managing a milk plant in Peekskill under the name Levi Trenton. Next, in July of 1918, we find multiple sexual harassment charges filed against a Leonard Tilton at a hat factory in Danbury, Connecticut. In January of this year, he failed an inspection of his payroll books that revealed excessive daily work hours and withheld wages under the name of Louis Tremaine in Yonkers."

Al pinched the skin between his eyes and waved his stogie at Miss Wald. "What kind of fools does this guy take us for? Does he think we've learned nothing from the Triangle Shirtwaist Factory fire? I ran for governor on the platform of establishing fair, safe working conditions. It's like this imposter is trying to rub our noses in the very reforms and regulations that Frances Perkins, Richard Wagner, and I fought tooth and nail for years to get passed!"

Miss Wald then turned to me. "And here, Miss McKenna, is where you come in. Explain what you've discovered, Ruth."

"This past March, Al's business and labor regulation department received an application for a permit to open a new factory in Brewster." Ruth passed an application to Miss Wald and indicated with her index finger a section near the bottom of the document. "Look at the list of names under the administrative positions."

"Well, I'll be doggoned." Miss Wald passed the application to me. The manager position at the factory was listed as one Lester Tussman.

Al leaned over and tapped me on my forearm. "I made Lillian here aware of the investigation you did on the homes for unwed mothers that led you to your sister. I also shared with her the invaluable work you performed during your internship with me in Albany."

I smirked. "I fetched coffee and sandwiches for your staff. I'd hardly call that investigative journalism."

"Never sell yourself short, Miss McKenna," said Miss Wald. "We have men to devalue our skills, and they do a fine job of it without our help. Isn't that right, Al?" She winked.

Al shrugged. "I'm outnumbered, ladies."

Miss Wald continued. "Ruth has shared with me your nose for fact finding and undercovering responsible parties, as you expertly demonstrated at the—" She read off the paper she was holding. "The Haviland Seminary for Girls, correct?"

I blushed. I never thought of putting my solving the mystery of Violet's suicide on a resume.

"Your qualifications at such a tender age make you the perfect candidate for this position," Al said. "You're sharp, intelligent, but innocent-looking enough so that no one will be the wiser if you apply for part-time work in this factory that has recently opened up in your hometown."

"Pardon me, but what type of factory is it, exactly? I know pretty much every storefront on Main Street."

Miss Wald glanced down again at the application. "Hoyas and Sons, Inc. It's a cigar factory."

My hand flew to my mouth.

"Jay, what's the matter?" asked Ruth.

"My sister works there. And I go to school with Pilar Hoyas. She's staying at Fowler House. She told me her father opened a cigar factory in Brewster."

Al clapped his hands and grinned. "Even better. Your sister and your friend can get you in the door, kid. You'll be able to get all sorts of inside information about the goings-on in the factory." He ticked off on his fingers. "Health code violations, hours of operation, labor relations, suppliers, machine safety regulations. Everything will be at your fingertips since you know the owner's daughter." He rubbed his hands together. "We'll have this creep behind bars in no time. He may think I'm still the uneducated mick from the Fulton Fish Market, but I've memorized every piece of legislation I can get my hands on up in Albany. This guy's going down, with your help, kid."

"But I'll feel like such a sneak. I'll be using my sister and knowingly withholding knowledge that Pilar's father hired a crook to manage one of the factories he opened in New York. Won't she become suspicious, and angry when she finds out the real reason I want to work in her father's factory?" Pilar had been through enough with the Gilded Lilies snub. She'd never trust me if she found out I was a spy.

"How well do you know this Pilar?" asked Ruth.

"Well enough. She's in all my classes, and she sleeps two beds over from me in the attic, I mean dormitory."

"She means attic," Ruth said drily.

"Can she be trusted?" asked Miss Wald.

I widened my eyes. "You mean you want to bring her in on this?"

Miss Wald shrugged. "Possibly. And what about your sister? Will she help you?"

"No way!" Eileen would kill me once she found out what I was up to."

"Don't worry about that," said Al, now pacing the floor of the office, rubbing his chin as he made his plans. "I think it's a great idea. I'll get in touch with your Pilar's father and bring him in on the whole operation. Ruth, can you hand me that license application?" He scratched his head. "And I can get my hands on some fine stogies as well!"

This was getting more exciting by the minute. "What about Florence? Ruth? Al? You know she would be excellent at this sort of operation."

Ruth pressed the palms of her hands together and rested her chin upon them. "Would Leonard Tussman hire a black girl to work in his cigar factory?"

"Probably not," said Miss Wald. "Unless the owner's daughter vouched for her." She raised her eyebrows and nodded her head, clearly impressed with her cleverness. "My, my. This is all falling into place quite nicely, I must say."

There was a light tap on the door. Miss Wald called, "Come in, Virginia."

Miss DeLuca poked her head in the door. "Your one o'clock is here."

Miss Wald stood. "Show Miss Federici in, please. I'd like to introduce her to Miss McKenna."

A slight, petite girl around my age entered the room. Her wide-spaced deep brown eyes revealed what Mam

136

would call "an old soul." She had dark lines under those eyes, as if she was tired or overworked. Her dark hair, flecked with auburn, was softly curled and pinned at the nape of her neck. Three beauty marks graced her right cheek. Her full lips were cracked. She dressed as a domestic, possibly a cook or maid. I could have sworn I'd seen her face before, but I couldn't place her.

"Constantina Federici, meet Josephine McKenna, your new apprentice for our next joint mission with Miss Lefkowitz. I want you to teach Josephine everything she will need to successfully work undercover in a cigar factory. I believe she has the stuff you're made of."

"I'll do what I can, but I've never gone undercover in a cigar factory," said Constantina.

Al offered her a chair. "We don't mean the technical aspects of the job itself. Miss McKenna is bright; she'll pick it up quick enough. I'm referring to the strategies you use to gather information without raising suspicion."

"Of course, Governor Smith." Constantina nodded, rubbing her eyes as she struggled to stay awake.

"You look exhausted, dear," said Miss Wald. "I'll have Cook fix you a cup of tea and something to eat. How's progress in the trouser factory?"

Constantina brightened a bit. "It's only a matter of time before the whole operation is shut down, Miss Wald. I've just come off a twelve-hour shift on my feet with no meal or necessary-room breaks. Thank goodness I don't have to go back in tonight. The male workers work eight-hour shifts with meals and breaks. The Italian and Jewish girls who don't speak English work the longer shifts, and they have to ask, in English, to use the toilet facilities. No chairs are provided at the sewing machine work stations. I have a signed petition from the other machine operators and lower management that the place is a firetrap. Inadequate ventilation, lighting, trash disposal, sanitary facilities, you name it. I'm confident we have enough to send Miss Lefkowitz's city and state safety inspectors in later today or tomorrow."

Al threw his hands up in the air. "It's like my regulations mean nothing! These corrupt factory owners are flaunting their violations in our faces, Ruth!" He slapped his hand down on the desk in frustration. "Jay, I suggest you spend the night with Constantina in her boardinghouse. Get to know how a typical factory girl lives, or rather, survives. We'll have you back on the train to Carmel tomorrow. Miss Federici, can you show our Jay the ropes? I want to double our efforts shutting down these unscrupulous factory owners all over the state who put their workers' lives in danger. We have the funding. I made sure of that when I increased the state budget. I've heard enough!"

Ruth stared at Constantina for a few moments. "Excuse me, Miss Federici, have we met?"

Constantina grinned shyly. "Possibly."

"I thought the same thing, Ruth," said Al, peering into Constantina's eyes. "You look awful familiar."

Constantina shrugged. "I must have that kind of face."

Al and Miss Wald had to leave to attend a meeting reviewing the number of influenza cases reported by various New York City hospitals and agencies during the previous year's Spanish flu epidemic. Miss Wald showed us the total number, a staggering 10,419 people. Constantina had to get a few hours' sleep back at her boardinghouse, so Ruth gave me a tour of the Henry Street Settlement House and introduced me to the staff. I had to fill out a job application, as I would be paid jointly by her office and Miss Wald's. I was so excited about going undercover that I hadn't realized I was actually going to get paid for it.

Chapter Eight

"This is the address Lillian gave me," said Ruth as I pulled the car up to Constantina's boardinghouse on Twenty-Fourth Street that evening. A nun in full black habit was sweeping the brownstone steps. A second was raking shriveled brown leaves in a tiny square garden.

"I didn't know boardinghouses were run by nuns," I said, after Constantina came to the set of double doors to let us in.

Constantina chortled. "Mama forbid me from staying in a boardinghouse when I arrived in New York, unless it was run by the Catholic Church and barred men from stepping through the front door. She already thinks it's a disgrace I'm living on my own after earning enough to move out of my brother's tenement."

Ruth introduced herself to the tall, somber nun standing behind Constantina and pressed an envelope into her hand. "You have Miss Lillian Wald's assurance that Miss McKenna will only be staying for the night. I will be by to pick her up in the morning."

"As long as Miss McKenna obeys our rules of no male visitors, quiet observed at all times, no profanity or using the Lord's name in vain, and a ten o'clock lights-out policy, she is welcome to stay for the night. I've arranged for a cot to be made up in Miss Federici's room. We do not provide meals, but Miss Federici has kitchen privileges and the use of a shared bathroom on the second floor."

"Agreed," I answered. These were far better living conditions than I was accustomed to at Fowler House. As a bonus, I didn't smell any cats.

"I'm afraid it isn't much," Constantina said as we entered a small bedroom, sparsely furnished with a single bed, a white iron headboard, a crucifix draped with rosary beads affixed to the wall, and a modest chest of drawers upon which sat a brush, comb and hand mirror arranged on a lace doily.

"Oh, how lovely." I pointed to a radiator that must have been installed during the Victorian era. It had lovely raised decorative designs in the cast iron. Two camisoles were laid over the top, to dry, I assumed.

"You'll find it's not so lovely when it's clanking and hissing steam before daybreak tomorrow morning," Constantina remarked.

I almost snickered. What we girls in the Fowler's damp, drafty attic wouldn't give for a radiator to warm our beds.

A small braided rug was the only other adornment in the spotlessly clean room. My cot, which was a true and proper bed with a mattress on wheels, was pushed against the wall opposite Constantina's. I could smell the freshly laundered white sheets and pillowcase. I hadn't slept in a bed so inviting since I left for school in September.

"I think it's wonderful. I share a leaky attic with eleven other girls in a house overrun with cats and squirrels wearing knitted bonnets."

"What?" Constantina cried. "Squirrels wearing bonnets? You're joking, surely."

"I'm serious. This place seems like Kensington Palace to me." I dropped my valise on the floor and lay down upon my bed, sinking into the heavenly softness of an eiderdown quilt scented with lavender.

"Don't get too comfortable." Constantina pulled me up off the bed. "We have a lot of work to cover. First, though, we eat. I'm starving."

We went downstairs to the simple but well-appointed kitchen off the main hallway. Constantina made herself at home, taking a tray of pasta she called cavatelli from the ice box. "I made them yesterday before I started my shift at the waist factory, so this shouldn't take long at all."

I watched her perform culinary magic with some stalks of broccoli and a bulb of garlic she had picked up at her cousin's greengrocers on her way home.

"Jay, can you pump some water over at the sink and set it to boiling on the stove?"

"Will this pot do, Constantina?" I asked, taking the largest one, dented, but still okay, hanging from a rack on the wall.

"Perfect, and please call me Tina. Now the first thing you want to do when you apply for the position at the cigar factory is fit in, or better yet, be invisible. Don't flaunt your education. That will be a red flag for your employer. Act meek, inexperienced, and grateful for whatever lousy pay this scumbag, Larry Tassone, or whatever name he calls himself these days, offers you."

Tina trimmed the stems and handed me the broccoli once the water came to a boil. "Boil these for three minutes. The next thing you want to remember is keep your mouth shut. No one will be forthcoming if you voice your opinions. If Larry Tassone insults you, mistreats you, or cheats you, take it. Keep a small pad and pencil hidden in your camisole. Use your lavatory breaks to take notes on every infringement he commits. Log the dates, times, and exact locations. Be objective, almost scientific, in your descriptions of what happened. Don't let your feelings affect what you log, because the courts will dismiss your findings and attribute them to female hysteria."

She started slicing three cloves of garlic on a cutting board. When three minutes passed, she handed me a large colander. "Take the broccoli stalks off the flame and strain them in this."

I passed the drained broccoli to Tina and watched as she cut the stalks into bite-size pieces with kitchen shears. "Now fill that pot up again and boil the cavatelli for the same amount of time."

"The whole tray?" I asked. She nodded and I did as she asked.

"Now, as hard as it may seem, if Tassone flirts with or even touches a coworker, don't object, just log it."

"But my best friend, Florence, will be working with me. How can I keep silent?"

"You'll do her far better if you stay quiet and log every detail you can recall so you can submit it to Mrs. Lefkowitz as evidence."

When I hesitated, Tina responded, "This is not a job for the fainthearted. Are you sure you're up for this?"

"I have to explain to Florence and Pilar what they're signing up for. I have nothing to lose, but they do. I don't want Florence to be subjected to prejudice or inappropriate behavior, and I don't want to trick Pilar into doing something that may put her father out of business. Being invisible comes naturally for me, but I want my friends to know the whole story before I involve them." I was haunted by Mary Agnes and what she told me last April. Look at all the harm she caused by being invisible.

"Fair enough. As long as you're in, talk to your friends so they have a clear picture about what is at risk if they take part in this. Now drain the cavatelli while I sauté the garlic in this big frying pan. Hand me the olive oil, will you?"

I took a bottle of golden olive oil from the counter and passed it to Tina, who used it to coat the bottom of the heavy black cast iron pan. The smell of the garlic frying in the oil was mouthwatering. Tina then added the cavatelli and broccoli to the pan and added a little of the pasta water she saved. She divided what was in the pan into two bowls, drizzled a little more olive oil on top of each bowl of pasta, and sprinkled some pecorino Romano cheese as a finishing touch. She handed me a loaf of bread while she grabbed two jelly glasses from the cupboard.

"Slice this good semolina bread, Jay, and grab the butter from the icebox. I'll pour the vino."

"Mangia," she announced as she set the bowls down on the small kitchen table covered in a red checkered oilcloth.

I found the utensils drawer and set two places with white cloth napkins. I brought the sliced bread on a cutting board and a dish of fresh churned butter to the table. Tina poured rich red wine into the glasses from a jug she kept behind the curtain under the sink.

"Won't the sisters object to the wine?" I asked, taking a bite of what was, beyond a doubt, the most delicious meal I'd ever eaten.

Tina chuckled as she sipped her wine. "My cousin Frank buys the flowers the sisters cut from their gardens to sell in his greengrocers, and he pays them with his homemade table wine in a type of bartering system. The nuns love his wine because it reminds them of home, so they don't give me a hard time about drinking it with dinner. Frank gives them the same family discount he gives me on his produce."

"You are an amazing cook, and I can see why Miss Wald scooped you up right away as a domestic. How did you get into undercover work? Don't you miss your family back in Italy? What made you decide to come to America? Alone, at that?" I dunked my bread to soak up the sauce Tina created with the pasta water.

"You ask a lot of questions, Jay. Make sure not to do that when you get a job at the cigar factory." Tina took a small sip from her glass. "First off, I had to leave Sicily because there was nothing there for me. My father promised me to a man twice my age, so my mother scheduled my ship fare here. Papa knows better than to mess with Mama, so he didn't prevent me from leaving. Second, my cousin Frank and his wife, Mimma, welcomed me with open arms when I arrived, even though they were raising four children in a tenement. I earned my keep by watching the little ones while Frank, Mimma, and their eldest son worked at their greengrocers. They referred me to Henry Street Settlement House to learn English, and I must have impressed the instructor, because she recommended me as a domestic to Miss Wald. I guess Miss Wald studied me while I did her mending and cooking. She asked me if I was interested in posing as an Italian immigrant working in a shirtwaist factory managed by man who was not adhering to the laws Governor Al Smith had passed in legislature. I jumped at the chance. Once I proved myself, she sent me on undercover missions to other garment factories and homes for unwed—"

"That's it!" I set my glass down, spilling a little on the tablecloth. I mopped it up quickly with my napkin. "That's where I saw you. You were the young nun when I went to rescue Eileen. What was her name again? Sister Albertine!"

Tina smiled as she swallowed a bite of the delicacy she created with her own hands. "I was so very impressed with your fire, Jay. Not even Mother Superior would keep you from your sister."

I playfully snapped my napkin at her arm. "Why didn't you say something earlier? I've been driving myself crazy trying to figure out where I've seen you before. Ruth and Al recognized you as well."

Tina laughed. "Please apologize to them for me. I was trying to test your powers of observation, Jay. You'll need to have a sharper sense of recall when you work undercover at the factory. You'll have to remember faces, details, and times until you can write them down in your log. Commit everything to memory. It's important in this line of work."

"Dates won't be a problem." That's how I figured out that Mary Agnes was the one who figuratively pushed Violet to her death. "Faces and details I'll have to work on."

Constantina chuckled and then said, "I'll never forget the look on Sister Benedicta's face when Governor-elect Al Smith came through the door. You have some friends in high places! That was one for the books." She slapped her thigh. "Oh, but I did catch some heat from Miss Wald for telling Eileen to run to you. Here I am going on about observing, not acting. I didn't think. I just wanted Eileen to be with you."

"I'll be forever grateful to you for sending her back to us." I stopped and thought about running through the slushy streets of Manhattan that day, desperate to find my sister. "So Sister Albertine was working undercover, not even a real nun. You're good, Tina. You had me convinced you were trapped in there like the girls, bullied by that awful Mother Superior. I thought you were a bit daft for staying there. I wanted a hot cup of tea so bad, but you said you weren't allowed in the kitchen by yourself. However did you pull it off?"

"Well, it helped that the sisters who ran the home for unwed mothers were from the same order as the sisters who run this boardinghouse, Sisters of the Divine Providence. When I told the nuns here what I was about to do, they contacted Miss Wald and agreed to work with her. They lent me a habit and gave me a crash course in how to behave like a novice nun. The most important skill I had to maintain was obedience, which was not easy with my Sicilian temper, believe me. The sisters knew of Sister Benedicta, and they contacted The Mother House to inform them of how she was mismanaging the home. She's spending an indefinite amount of time at The Mother House, reflecting, shall we say." Tina snickered as she refilled our glasses.

By the time my head hit the soft pillow around midnight, I was well versed in the ways of working undercover in a factory. I only had to put what Tina taught me into practice, and I might escape the cigar factory without two bullets in my head, one from Larry Tassone and one from Pilar's father.

*

MONDAY, NOVEMBER 3, 1919

"Let me get this straight. You want my father to know-ingly keep someone on as manager who has rigged books, denied pay, harassed employees, and ignored safety regu-lations in at least five other places under assumed names? And you expect me to get you a job there so you can spy on him until you've got enough evidence of wrongdoing that will probably shut down my father's place of business? Are you mad?" Pilar got up from the bench we were sitting on in the courtyard outside the dining hall. She paced back and forth among the burgundy leaves whirling across the grass on this windy day. Autumn had set ablaze the Japanese red maple trees, and now they were in their fiery crimson glory. This was their swan song, for by the end of the month, they'd be bare. "You've got to see that this is the most harebrained scheme you've ever come up with."

Up until this point, Florence, Pilar, and I had been en-joying one of our last lunches outside before cold weather would force us back into the overcrowded dining hall. A squirrel was nibbling on rotting apples, paying no mind to three gray doves enjoying a bite for themselves.

"I wish Ruth and Miss Wald could be here to explain the plan to you in person. I know I'm making it sound crazy," I said. "But if you could just hear me out even though I'm not expressing myself very well."

Pilar had returned from her pacing by this point. "I don't see how it can get much worse."

"I met a girl named Tina, an Italian immigrant, who rose from a maid to an undercover agent for Lillian Wald, who runs the Henry Street Settlement. Turns out, she was posing as a nun when I went to rescue my sister from the home for unwed mothers that my father forced her to enter. Tina made it possible for Eileen to return to us. She's dedicated her life to documenting information on people who mistreat women. She gave me a little training on how to remain invisible while observing the wrongdoings of people in positions of authority. I can't carry this off without the two of you."

"What's wrong with just letting my father know Larry Tassone misrepresented himself so he can fire him?" asked Pilar.

"He's slick enough to escape prosecution by leaving town the minute authorities get wind of his illegal activities. He changes his name, applies to manage a factory in a different town, and his filthy slate is wiped clean. He's confident that he's found a way to cheat and mistreat women and get away with it. If your father fires him, Pilar, he'll just go somewhere else. Don't you want to see him stopped?" I tried not to sound desperate.

"Not at the expense of my family. They've worked hard to build our business." Pilar jutted her chin out in a mix of pride and defensiveness. "My grandfather worked for the most famous cigar manufacturers out of Cuba, Vincente Ybor, until he left Key West for what was to become Ybor City in Tampa. My grandfather struck out on his own so he could keep his family in Key West among friends. My father built the business to the point that he could venture north. This is his chance to make a name in New York. The Brewster factory is one of five that can make or break the Hoyas name in the cigar industry.

Surely you can understand that I cannot risk my family's good name."

"Of course I understand. I'll call Ruth and tell her I can't accept the position." I said this even though I had no intention of contacting her.

Pilar came and sat beside me. "I'm sorry, Jay. I know you want to get this guy, but I can't deceive my father. Too much is riding on the success of this factory."

"It's okay. Ruth will have to understand." I stood to dump my tray, swallow my disappointment, and think of a way to get back into my friends' good graces until I could figure out how to get Pilar and Florence to join me on my undercover work.

"Hey, I have an idea. I got a letter from Henry this morning asking me to meet him at Smalley's for lunch after the Returning Veteran's parade Saturday. My brothers will be marching, and the American Legion will be holding a ceremony to receive all the soldiers. Why don't we all watch the parade and attend the luncheon together? Clara, Louise, and Eleanor can come along. There'll be plenty of cute guys there. It'll be fun."

Chapter Nine

"Here it is, Jay. Christopher F. McKenna." Florence found Christie's name on the monument the American Legion unveiled to honor Putnam County's soldiers lost in the war.

"Stand there, Jay, and let me get a picture," said Nancy, as she focused her Brownie camera. "Now you, Packy, get in there with your sister. Where's Jimmy Joe?" She shielded her eyes against the sun with her hand.

"Your sister-in-law looks so smart in her Red Cross uniform," said Clara. "Look at that fancy frog closure at the neck of her cape, and that stylish hat."

"I like her," I said. "She's modern and intelligent, and she certainly gives my mother a run for her money."

"Where is your mother?" asked Florence, shielding her eyes from the sun. "I'd like to meet her."

"She always finds excuses not to attend public events. She has the perfect reason now to stay home with the baby." I spotted Henry waving his arms from the doorway at Smalley's.

"I found a table, Jay! Come on in."

My friends and I made our way through the maze of

soldiers, high school bands, Girl Scouts, Boy Scouts, American Legion members, families of veterans (alive and dead), and guests.

"This is the biggest table I could find," said Henry. "The new owner, Ralph something or other, has put out quite a spread. Hungry?"

"Starved." We draped our Haviland coats across the seats at the coveted table and made our way to the buffet. The American Legion Military Band was playing John Philip Sousa marches.

"Well, well, well, look who's making his way to our table," Louise said as we were digging in to our roast beef sandwiches and potato salad.

Will was balancing two shot glasses in one hand and carrying a bottle under his arm. "Room for one more?" he asked.

I was sitting between Florence and Henry. "Can you move down a seat so Will can sit down? He's the boy who boards with us at Fowler House. I'll introduce you."

"Should I be jealous?" Henry glanced toward the six-foot, muscular build of Will as he moved our plates down a seat. "The girls must go crazy for him."

"He's only got eyes for Florence," I said.

"Uh, isn't that a little dangerous?" Henry whispered. "Folks around here don't take kindly to that sort of thing, if you know what I mean."

"I know what you mean," I whispered back. "They're just friends, really."

"They'd better be careful." Henry stood up and took his plate. "I'm going back for seconds. Hey, isn't that Eileen at the door? Who's that slick-looking fellow with her?"

"What's she doing with him?" I asked. "He's far too old for her."

Eileen waved like a film star and maneuvered her way through the tables. She was decked out in a fake beaver coat with a deep shawl collar and loose mandarin sleeves. Her newly styled short blond tendrils poked about from beneath a new helmet hat made of brown silk-faced velvet. "Jay, Packy, Nancy, I'd like you to meet Lester, Lester Tussman. Isn't he divine?"

"Pick your jaw up off the ground or you're going to blow your cover," Florence whispered into my ear.

I nodded and tried to regulate my breathing. There was no way in hell Eileen could be involved with this slimeball. My sister certainly had a nose for the losers.

Larry Tassone, aka Lester Tussman, shook all of our hands. I wiped mine with my napkin after he moved on to Packy. His jet-black hair was peppered with gray on the sides and slicked back with pomade. Above his thin lips was a thin mustache that could have been drawn on with a black oil crayon. His three-piece suit was checkered, well-tailored, and I almost choked on my sandwich when I saw he was wearing spats.

Larry whistled as he and Eileen seated themselves at our table. "Big family. You Irish breed like rabbits, don't you?" He guffawed loudly at his own joke, slapping his thigh. Nobody laughed back.

After reaching over to stuff a fistful of dollar bills in Eileen's hand, Larry brushed her off with a wave of his pinky-ringed hand. "Go grab us two drinks, baby."

I decided against telling him it was an open bar.

Nudging Will, who was deep in conversation with Florence, Larry said, "I guess we both know that Carmel's the place to come to when we want to go slumming, hey kid?" He erupted into another round of laughter, showing his huge white teeth.

Will stood up, glaring at Larry. He spoke through gritted teeth. "What do you mean by that?" His lips had turned white, and he was clenching his fists.

"Hey, he's not worth it, buddy. He's just a jerk," Henry said, standing and resting his hand on Will's arm.

Will wrenched Henry's hand off his arm and stood his ground. "No. I asked you a question, mister. We can settle it now or take it outside. Your choice."

Larry stood to his full height until he was chest-high to Will. Throwing his hands up, palms out, he snickered. "Calm down, fellow, I'm a lover, not a fighter. I get it. We all get a taste for the exotic once in a while, hey?" Leaning in to Will, he cupped his hand and whispered loudly, "I wouldn't mind a dish of that spicy senorita across the table," as he nodded toward Pilar, who blanched.

This time it was Henry who lunged across the table, grabbing both lapels of Larry's jacket. Henry pulled back his arm and clenched his fist. "If you want to keep those pearly whites of yours, it's time to beat it; now, mister."

"But I haven't had my drink yet," Larry protested as Will grabbed him by the back of his collar and forcibly pushed him through the crowd and out the door.

Eileen returned to the table with two whiskeys and looked at the empty chair. "What the— Where'd Lester go?" She narrowed her eyes at me and Packy. "What did you say to him?"

"Don't look at us," Packy said. He pointed to Will, who had just returned, red-faced and breathless from depositing Larry on the sidewalk. "He messed with the wrong guy."

"That creep makes Artie Tuttle seem like Rudolph Valentino, Eileen," I said, rising. "Drop him like a bad penny."

"He's my boss, you idiot!" Eileen yelled, slamming the drinks down on the table. "I could lose my job for this." She stormed away from the table, pushing people out of her way as she marched toward the door.

"When is she going to learn?" I asked Henry. "And she works for that creep."

"She does more than work for him," Nancy said. "Did you see that bracelet she was flaunting? Paste, probably, but how would Eileen know the difference with a smooth talker like that one?"

"He'll dump her as soon as someone else comes along," said Packy. "She never learns."

"And when he dumps her, she'll want revenge," said Pilar.

"What are you getting at?" I asked, curious.

"She probably has been promoted since she started at the cigar factory, since she's cozied up to the manager," Florence chimed in, giving me a knowing look.

"And she's more than likely privy to some confidential information," Pilar added. "Pillow talk and that type of thing."

"Pilar!" I shouted, embarrassed in front of the boys. "She's my sister, for heaven's sake. And what are you getting at, anyway?"

"Don't you see? Once Larry the Creep dumps Eileen, she can spill the beans on all his underhanded business dealings at the cigar factory," Florence explained.

"Papa's coming up this week to inspect the New York factories. I think you should meet with him to explain your plan. Florence, you come too. If Papa adamantly opposes your investigation, you will have to promise to stay out of it. If, however, he doesn't object to your involvement, you have my blessing."

"Really?" I asked. I had to admit I was shocked at her sudden change of heart.

"I've never been so insulted in my life, and by a grown man, at that. I want to see you take him down, Jay." Her eyes burned with indignation. "Don't mention the senorita remark to Papa. He'll shoot Larry on sight if he finds out the filth that came out of that man's mouth."

Thank you, Larry, for being disgusting enough to convince Pilar and Florence to join me in turning your sorry hide over to the law, I mouthed silently.

*

"Look at the delicious apple strudel and apple fritters. How are the pastry chefs at Smalley's able to make them with only that cruddy rainbow sugar available now?" I asked once the desserts and coffee were put out.

"They're all from Dieter's Confectionary," said Packy. "The new owner Ralph took on Old Fred Bailey as manager. Fred hired me and Jimmy Joe as dairy and produce providers and Dieter for bread and baked goods. Works out well all around!"

"Uh-oh." At the mention of the name Bailey, I locked eyes with Pilar. "We'd better keep an eye out for that nasty old relation of yours."

"I don't know, Jay. I might want to light up a nice, fat Havana after I enjoy all this delicious food," Pilar said, grinning.

Florence sighed and shook her head. "Here we go again."

"Uh-oh. Don't look now, but here comes trouble," said Packy. "Looks like Jimmy Joe got a head start at the bar."

I waved Jimmy Joe and Olive over to our table and instantly regretted doing so. My brother was walking a bit unsteadily.

"What's the matter with you?" I asked Olive, who was trembling and looked like she just saw a ghost.

"Uh, nothing," she said, a million miles away. "Honey, why don't you grab us some more drinks?" she said, resting her head on Jimmy Joe's shoulder. "I have to powder my nose."

Jimmy Joe kissed her hair. "Don't be long, sweetie."

"What are you doing with all these women?" Jimmy Joe slapped Packy on the back, hard, sending him off balance. Nancy steadied him.

"I guess you started the party without us, Jimmy Joe. Why don't you get something to eat?" Packy said, motioning for him to cut us in line at the buffet table.

"I don't need no crappy food. I'm going to the bar. They're giving out free drinks for veterans," slurred Jimmy Joe. "Let's get you away from the ball and chain for a little bit and throw back a few. What do you say, brother?" He belched loudly, causing Packy to take a step back.

"I'll meet you at the bar for a beer once I finish eating. You should eat too, from the look of it," said Packy. "Come on, just have a sandwich, Jimmy Joe. It's all on the house. Then we'll all join you and your lady friend for a drink." He nodded to Olive, who had just returned from the ladies' room.

"I wouldn't exactly call her a lady. Ain't that right, sweetie?" Jimmy Joe squeezed a glazed-eyed Olive tightly against him.

"I'll show you who's a lady," she growled, and clocked him over the head with her grungy old bag. Some of the contents of Olive's bag spilled onto the floor when she hit Jimmy Joe, who just laughed as they stumbled back to the bar.

"Let them go," said Packy. "He's just going to make a fool of himself, and I don't want to be around for that spectacle."

With plates piled high with pie and streusel, everyone started back for the table. I lagged behind.

"Can you take my plate back for me?" I asked Henry. "I want to pour a cup of tea. It was chilly watching the parade."

I returned to the spot they were standing in when Olive's bag spilled, knelt down, and picked up some loose change, cigarettes, and a used handkerchief. Reaching under the buffet stand to see if anything had rolled under it, my hand touched a small bottle. I grabbed it and brought it into the light. It was a medicine bottle. The name on the label was Morphine Sulfate. I shoved it into my pocket, poured my tea, and made my way back to my group.

"Nancy," I called down the table, "would you take a trip with me to the ladies' room?"

"Why do girls always have to go to the john in pairs?" asked Will. "It's not a very complicated mission."

Henry laughed. "You got me."

Nancy and I snaked our way around the crowded dining room until we reached the ladies' facilities. I stole a glance at the bar, where Jimmy Joe was entertaining the crowd with imitations of some of the politicians who attended the parade. Olive seemed to be fading, propping her head in her hand as she slumped against the bar top. Her lipstick was smeared, her eyes were drooping, and her hair was a mess.

"She looks like she's about to black out," said Nancy as we stood in line for the restroom.

"That's what I need to talk to you about," I said. "I don't

really need to use the bathroom. I want to show you something, in private."

"I don't have to go either. Let's step outside and walk down by the lake," she suggested.

"I know every inch of that lake by now," I said. "Let's get out of here."

I led Nancy to the spot near the boat where I hid my underwear the night I swam the length of the lake. Out of curiosity, I lifted the boat up and discovered they were gone. I would have loved to see the poor owner's face when he flipped over his boat and discovered this unique Halloween prank.

"What are you doing?" asked Nancy.

"It's a long story," I said. "I'll tell you about it when we go back in." I reached into the pocket of my dress and handed her the medicine bottle. "What is this?"

Nancy's raised her eyebrows as she read the label. "Where did you get your hands on this?" she asked suspiciously.

"It fell out of Olive's bag when she hit Jimmy on the head. I stayed behind and picked up her things. That rolled under the buffet stand."

"This is a highly addictive drug, used to treat pain from cancer. It is the number one drug among female addicts. If Olive is using this, she has a serious drug problem." Nancy opened the bottle and sniffed it. "Where on earth does she get this poison? It could kill her."

Like pieces of a puzzle, all of Olive's odd behaviors started to fit together. "She goes out for hours in the middle of the night. I saw her talking to some skanky-looking guy in the village a few weeks ago. Maybe she gets this drug from him." My mind started linking events to this bottle of morphine. "Once, Will found her sleeping standing up in the outhouse. She sleeps through class and picks at dry skin around her mouth and chin. She's very irritable, and she gets angry and lashes out at people for no reason. Oh, and I've had money stolen from my purse."

"Textbook morphine addiction, by the behaviors you've just described," said Nancy. "Her falling asleep standing up is what we refer to as 'on the nod' in the medical field. People who abuse opiates literally fall asleep while in the standing position." She held up the bottle. "Mind if I hold on to this? It's illegal to have this on your person without a prescription. I want to show it to Packy and Jimmy Joe before I dump the contents down the outhouse. This is dangerous stuff."

"Take it. But what do we do now?" I asked. "As I said, Olive has an explosive temper. She'll kill me if she finds out I took her morphine and gave it to you."

"She won't have the strength to kill a cat once she starts withdrawing from the drug. She'll find whatever lowlife is supplying her with this garbage so she can get more. I have to let Jimmy Joe know what he's up against. He's suffering enough without having to deal with her addiction." Nancy touched my arm. "You're a smart girl who knows how to handle herself. You'll figure out what to say to Olive when the time is right."

We turned and made our way back to Smalley's, and Nancy suddenly stopped at the entrance. "Mother! Father! What a surprise."

Nancy ushered her parents through the still-dense crowd and made introductions around the table. Mr. and Mrs. Outenhausen looked like a set of salt and pepper shakers painted as a farmer and his wife. Both were short and round. Mr. Outenhausen had a head of hair as white as salt. He wore a set of braces to hold his pants up across

his broad middle. His face was tanned and lined from decades of work in his apple orchards in Croton Falls. Mrs.
Outenhausen's wiry hair, pinned up in a bun, was still as
black as pepper, as were her eyes. She was sharp-witted
and in possession of a delightfully wicked sense of humor.
The couple perfectly complemented each other.

"Packy," said Nancy. "My parents wanted to see the
Veterans Monument. I wonder if the kitchen could send out
some more sandwiches and salad. There must be leftovers."

"Sure thing. You stay here with your folks. I'll go see
what they can rustle up in the kitchen. Be back in a jiffy."
Leaning on his cane, he made his way toward the kitchen.

"That boy's getting along well these days, I see," said
Mr. Outenhausen. Turning to his wife, he said, "Mother,
I see there's coffee and tea set up at the buffet table. Why
don't you help yourself while I go in search of something
a bit stronger?" His hooded green eyes had a mischievous
sparkle in them.

"Oh, go away with you, you old thing," kidded Nancy's
mother. "Can I bring anyone coffee?" She locked Nancy's
arm in hers as we approached a stack of cups and saucers.
"Now, let's have a good old-fashioned catching up back at
the table while your father searches for his gin and tonic,
shall we? How's that nasty old mother-in-law treating you?
Still grouchy as ever?"

"You're talking about Jay's mother, for heaven's sake!"
Nancy scolded.

I leaned over to Mrs. Outenhausen. "Still grouchy as
ever."

We shared a laugh while we were fixing more tea and
coffee when I spied Packy coming back from the kitchen
followed by the manager, who was holding two plates of
sandwiches and salads.

"Will you excuse me, Mrs. Outenhausen?" I raced back to the table to warn Pilar.

"Look!" I pointed to the old man who got us thrown out of Dieter's a few weeks ago.

"Leave it to me," said Pilar.

"Mrs. Outenhausen, how nice of you to come." The manager set the plates in front of her on the table. "I believe your husband does business with my brother, Herb Bailey. He manages the Brewster House. I just took over as manager here at Smalley's. Name's Fred Bailey. I buy milk and produce from Packy, here. He said you're his new in-laws. Congratulations. I hope you'll make yourself at home. Let me know if you need anything."

Mr. Bailey was exchanging pleasantries with Nancy's mother when Pilar came around the table and stood by his side.

"May I help you, young lady?" he asked. He hesitated a minute before his eyes widened in recognition. He stood, frozen.

"I heard your name, Mr. Bailey. Perhaps you know my mother, the former Grace Bailey?"

Fred Bailey stuttered, clearly dumbfounded. "Why, yes, I, uh, it's been years since, uh, Grace was my brother Hugh's youngest girl."

"Yes, she is. I didn't have an opportunity to introduce myself the last time we met. I believe it was at Dieter's. Do you recall that day a few months ago, Uncle Fred?"

"Why, yes, I, I think I do." He stumbled, looking at the floor and shuffling his feet.

"Good, well now that we've been properly introduced, I'll write Mama and tell her how well received I've been by her family since my arrival. Good day, Uncle Fred." She smiled and returned to her seat.

"Yes, well, then, I hope you all help yourselves to whatever you'd like. Drinks are on the house all day. Good day." He tipped his hat and shuffled back to the kitchen, tail between his legs.

I had Nancy's mother and the rest of our table in stitches as Florence and I did our best impressions of Fred Bailey's rampage after Pilar lit up a cigar in Dieter's, when Nancy looked up, surprised.

"Father, what is it?"

Mr. Outenhausen reached for his wife's chair with his work-hardened hands. His voice sounded shaky. "Mother, you'd better come with me. There's someone in the bar I want you to take a close look at." He had a stricken look on his weathered face.

"Who did you see, dear?" Mrs. Outenhausen patted the chair next to her. "Sit down for a minute. You look like you've had a fright." She turned to Nancy. "Perhaps you could bring us a glass of water."

Nancy returned with a glass of water in a flash. She bent down and took her father's hands. "Your pulse is racing, Father. Tell us who you saw at the bar that gave you such a start."

Mr. Outenhausen took a sip of water to compose himself. With shaky hands, he replaced the glass on the table and began. "Mother, do you recall in September when that girl showed up on our doorstep asking for a place to stay the night?"

"What a ridiculous question. How could I possibly forget the day that wretched beast took advantage of our kindness and took off like the thief she was with five hundred dollars' worth of jewelry, liberty bonds, and cash? She wiped us out, and got away with the lot of it."

"Well, you'd better prepare yourself, Mother, because

I believe I just saw her in the bar, nearly passed out, but I'll never forget that girl's face as long as I live. I think it's her."

My blood turned cold as Nancy and I exchanged looks.

"They always turn to stealing to support their habit," she whispered in my ear.

"Father, show me this girl at once!" demanded Mrs. Outenhausen. "Nancy, find a phone and ring the police. Oh, never mind. I see Officer Belden at a table with his family. Fetch him, please." She rose and took her husband's arm. "Take me to her now."

I followed behind, dreading this encounter. Henry, Will, Florence, Pilar, and the rest of our friends joined me. Once we made our way to the bar, Mr. Outenhausen pointed to Olive, draped across the bar, nodding off while Jimmy Joe clinked beer mugs and sang army songs with his buddies.

Mrs. Outenhausen approached Olive, studying her face. "Thief!" she screeched. "Officer Belden, arrest this woman, now! She robbed my home!"

Officer Belden blew his whistle and chaos erupted. I watched as Jimmy Joe sprang into action, grabbing a startled Olive and sprinting out the back door of the bar, while his buddies started throwing punches to throw the police officer off course. Chairs were strewn across the floor to block his path and give Jimmy Joe and Olive time to escape. The bar erupted into a full donnybrook that spilled out into the street.

Officer Belden blew his whistle again, longer and shrill enough for the patrons in the dining hall to cover their ears. "This bar is closed, and this function is officially ended. Go back to your homes and stay there until morning! That's an order!" The buttons on his uniform jacket looked about ready to pop.

We gathered our things and made our way toward the front door, where Fred Bailey was waving his arms frantically.

"Don't go, please stay!" he cried, blocking the door. "I'll talk sense into Officer Belden! This is our busiest day ever! Drinks are on the house until closing! Everything's on the house until closing! Please!"

Pilar unwrapped a fat cigar and clipped the end as she walked by him. "Got a light, Uncle Fred?"

*

MONDAY, NOVEMBER 24, 1919
HOYAS AND SONS CIGAR FACTORY
BREWSTER, NEW YORK

"I'm still not convinced this is the best way to go about things, but I'll give you two weeks, and if there's one bit of trouble, I expect you to contact me immediately, Maria del Pilar. Do I make myself understood?" Javier Hoyas was a well-built man with the same jet-black hair as his daughter, Pilar. He wore a stiff new collar with a bow tie and a well-tailored three-piece dark wool suit. His accent was clipped, but slight, wanting to make the best impression with his financial backers in New York.

"Yes, Papa. We've been over the logistics for two weeks." Pilar reminded her father how Lillian Wald invited all of us, including Mr. Hoyas, to Delmonico's in the city to explain how the entire operation would proceed. Miss Wald emphasized how crucial it was for us to collect enough evidence and have Larry Tassone arrested before he got away like he had from the last five factories he worked in. Al Smith met with Mr. Hoyas up in Albany to assure him that his factories were under the protection of the New

York State Government throughout the entire investigation and subsequent court hearings.

"I watched you both shake on it, Papa," Pilar continued. "You have his personal phone number, for goodness sake. How much more assurance do you need that this is safe?"

When Mr. Hoyas hesitated, I added, "The local, county, and state police have been alerted and are on call. You simply have to pick up the phone and call Lillian when I let you know Florence and I have enough evidence."

"I don't know. To put innocent young girls at risk is not how we operate where I come from. My own daughter could get hurt, even though she won't be working here in the factory. And you, my dear." He gently wagged his finger as he addressed Florence. "In Key West, Cubans of every shade work side by side in the factories. We have Cuban Afro floor managers, supervisors, owners. We all belong to the same social clubs." He struck a match and puffed on his cigar for a few moments before continuing. "Up north, they pretend to be more tolerant than the South, but I can see for myself how dark-skinned people are treated here. There is not the equality that Cubans enjoy in Key West. I will not tolerate a young girl being mistreated based on the color of her skin, so help me!"

I watched a thin film of sweat gathering on Mr. Hoyas's brow despite the damp chill in his cigar factory office. A low fire in the grate did little to warm the room.

"Papa," Pilar said in a voice dripping with charm, "I understand that you do not want me working here, but I've had an idea."

I tried to warn Pilar with my stare that this was not the time to ask her father for more involvement when he was still so far from being sold on the whole idea. Clearly, I was not effective.

"You know the storytellers that read to cigar rollers back home?" she asked in wide-eyed innocence.

"Yes, and the stories they used to read have become more political—ranting about labor unions and rebellion. It won't be long before they're banned altogether, if I have anything to say about it."

I closed my eyes and prepared for defeat. Florence shook her head and sighed. Why was Pilar deliberately trying to railroad this whole operation?

"Well, Papa, I wasn't thinking anything along those lines, of course. Rather, since the majority of your employees in this factory are women, I was wondering if maybe they would enjoy hearing someone read from the classics...Shakespeare, for instance, or Jane Austen. Maybe something from the Bronte sisters or Jay's favorite, Louisa May Alcott?"

"Don't get me wrapped up in this," I protested.

"You're already wrapped up in this, Jay." Pilar turned to her father. "Surely you wouldn't object to entertaining our employees during their long hours with a bit of culture?"

Mr. Hoyas leaned forward in his chair, propped his elbows on his desk, and rested his head in his hands. "And who, pray tell, were you thinking of asking to read to the workers?"

"I wouldn't ask anyone, Papa. I would volunteer to come in a few times a week and read to the workers myself." Butter wouldn't melt in her mouth at this point.

Mr. Hoyas then covered his face with his hands and shook his head. When he had sufficiently calmed, he walked to his door and summoned his secretary. "Miss Hohenrath, who's the floor manager today?"

Miss Hohenrath reminded me of a fairy. She was petite,

with sparkling blue eyes and short blond hair. She must have trained as a ballet dancer, for she walked with her feet pointed out and stood in first position. I thought I might have spotted a trace of pixie dust on her upturned nose.

"It's that Miss McKenna, I'm afraid. She's excellent at her job, sir. I just don't condone mixing business with pleasure. Draw your own conclusions, Mr. Hoyas."

Mr. Hoyas removed his horn-rimmed glasses and pinched the skin above his nose with his thumb and forefinger. "I don't have time to deal with this. I've a train to catch."

"Of course, sir." She placed several sheets of paper and train tickets on his desk. "Here is your travel itinerary to Grand Central, complete with all your connections and transfer train tickets to Miami, then the railroad down to Key West. I'll wager you're anxious to get home, Mr. Hoyas."

"Thank you, Miss Hohenrath. Please instruct Miss McKenna to give these young ladies a tour of the rooms." He motioned for Florence and me to follow Miss Hohenrath. "I'll leave Miss Eileen McKenna to your discretion."

"Very good, sir. I'll summon Miss McKenna now. Will that be all?"

"Yes." After checking the time, he replaced a gold pocket watch hanging from a chain in his vest pocket. "I'll be taking dinner with my daughter at the Southeast House before catching the train. Mr. Tussman will be in in about an hour to resume his operation of the factory as manager. That'll be all. And girls..."

Florence and I turned around.

"One problem, you get me on the phone straight away, no matter what time. Understood?"

"Understood, sir," we answered in unison.

Eileen's stare dripped venom as Miss Hohenrath instructed her to give Florence and me a tour of the factory.

"What the hell are you doing here?" she snarled after Miss Hohenrath returned to her desk outside Mr. Hoyas's office. She dug her fingernails into my forearm. "Go home, and take your friend with you."

I yanked my arm away and rubbed it. "My friend Pilar's father owns this factory, and Florence and I need to earn spending cash for Christmas. Mr. Hoyas said we could come on board as seasonal help, as there's typically a rush on cigars for the holidays. You can pretend you don't know me, but we need the wages. Now just tell us what to do and put us to work. I'll stay out of your hair, promise."

Eileen hesitated for a moment. "One month, or a bit more. You're both out before Christmas. And I don't know either of you. I want to keep this promotion, and you're not going to ruin it for me. I've got my eye on a permanent management position. And Jay, I get fifty percent of your salary."

"Fifty percent?" I wailed. "That's highway robbery."

"Sixty percent. Take it or leave it."

"Oh, okay," I sighed, trying to sound convincing. Eileen had no idea that Florence and I were getting paid by both Miss Wald's and Ruth's offices. I was enjoying this part of our undercover work. "What do we have to do?"

"First come with me." Eileen led us into a drafty room, bare except for a long, rough-hewn table wedged in between two benches of equal length. On one wall was a line of shelves and coat hooks. "This is where you hang your coats and leave your dinner pails."

Florence and I found two adjacent hooks and proceeded

to change into the smocks we brought from painting class.

"Not there." Eileen pointed to Florence. "What's your name?"

"It's Florence, ma'am," she murmured, her eyes cast downward in feigned deference. I'd never seen Florence take such a subservient tone. She was some good actress.

"Your spot is down here at the end." Eileen directed Florence to a coat hook far from mine. My friend silently obeyed. My sister ignored the quizzical look I shot her.

"Since you know nothing, you'll have to start at the bottom, here in the stripping and booking room. Come on, let's get started." She opened the door to the workroom.

Although almost every chair was occupied, the concrete-walled room was silent. The air was heavy with the potent smell of raw tobacco, reminiscent of a campfire after someone dumped a bucket of water over it to douse the flames. I thought I could also detect the scent of skunk, knowing that smell only too well since Sullivan was sprayed by one over the summer. The damp chill permeated my skin straight to the bone, prompting me to rub my upper arms for warmth. How could I ever sit here for hours after school and on weekends? I hoped we would quickly get as much evidence as possible to secure Larry Tassone's arrest so we could leave this hellhole.

Eileen grabbed my arm and roughly guided me over to an empty chair. Florence stood behind us to watch.

"The workers in this room prepare the tobacco leaves for the hands of the cigar makers in the next room." She picked up a large smelly leaf from a pile on the table and demonstrated for us. "The large center stem is stripped out like this." She deftly removed the thick stem. "Lester said the reason I've taken to this so naturally is because my hands are so delicate and used to making tiny invisible stitches in my sewing. You're going to have a rough time with those big beefy hands of yours, Jay." She looked up at Florence. "Show me your hands."

Florence obliged, holding her hands out for inspection.

"You'll do better. Your hands are nice and feminine, not manly like Jay's."

Tina's warning echoed in my ears. I had to take every insult, rude comment, and violation of worker's rights lying down, even if they came from Eileen, or I'd be found out. I thanked Florence with a nod for her passive response to Eileen's demand, for I had shared Tina's instructions with both her and Pilar once we were somewhat sure that Mr. Hoyas would acquiesce to our plan.

"Now, pay attention, you two." I could see how much Eileen enjoyed schooling us. It was her revenge for my having to help her with homework on the days she decided to show up for school. "Once you remove the center stem, you have to inspect the tobacco leaf to make sure it is of the finest quality for making cigar wrappers. There can be no rot, no evidence of disease whatsoever. A worker was fired last month for trying to pass off a cigar, which upon close inspection was filled with whatever was swept off the floor. This type of counterfeit could get the factory shut down, so if you see that happening, you're honor bound to report that to Lester, I mean, the manager, Mr. Tussman."

I became slightly nauseous thinking of my pretty, young sister with that pig.

"Now, the two of you will start out just stripping out the stems and inspecting the leaves for now. Once you have a pile of stripped, clean leaves, you pass them off to a booker, who will smooth each leaf tightly across her knee and roll it into a compact pad ready for a cigar maker's table in the room next door. Only men are allowed in there, so you are not to leave this room. Now," she continued, "in the highly unlikely event that either of you show any promise in booking your own wrapper, you will be paid three dollars a week for stripping and booking your own leaves. I will be the judge of that, so don't go trying to show off, just to try to elevate yourself to the position of Booker Stripper."

I bit my tongue to stifle a laugh at the name, for it conjured up the image of a well-read girl working in a bawdy house.

"Now, Jay, you stay here, and your friend—Florence—can take a seat over there in the back row. Remember, no talking allowed, take your dinner break when everyone else does, and don't speak to me unless you need to use the necessary room. Raise your hand and don't leave your seat until I tell you to."

Tina had instructed us to wear our shabbiest clothes, and still we were overdressed in the smocks we used for our art elective. I recognized many girls seated throughout the rows in the room, yet no one acknowledged me with even a nod. I made a mental note of this. Larry Tassone ran a tight ship. Mabel Pugsley, whom I saw Artie Tuttle flirt with at Dieter's Confectionary several times throughout the time he courted Eileen, was bent over her work. I instantly felt mean-spirited for having that be the first thought that entered my head regarding Mabel, for her mother had succumbed to the Spanish flu a little over a year ago, and her father had since fallen on hard times. Henry told me Mabel had quit school once she found work in this cigar factory.

Everyone else looked vaguely familiar, but I had been so out of touch with the village since I left for Haviland that I had trouble placing names on the rows of bent heads. Florence, I observed, was not the only dark-complected worker in the room. There were two others, and they were both seated in the back row alongside Florence. The factory was segregated. Not unusual, but I made my second mental note.

Larry Tassone entered the stripping and booking room about an hour into our work. He passed each girl, complimenting neat piles of leaves, reprimanding slow work paces, and instructing those with sloppy work areas to tidy up. I kept my head down, not eager to be recognized. He ignored Florence and the others in the back row. From the corner of my eye, I saw him place his hand lightly across Mabel's back as he passed her, in a swiping motion. It was so quick that it could have easily gone unnoticed if I wasn't looking for something. After he left the room, I noticed Mabel wiping a tear that was running down her cheek.

Stripping tobacco leaves was probably the most tedious job I had ever taken on, and I resented having to tell Mrs. Cornish I couldn't sweep up in her store for the time being. At least the work at the drug store allowed me time to chat with Betty's parents and the customers. The silence and mindless work in the factory made it a miserable way to earn a living. I would be glad to get out of there as soon as possible. There was no clock in the room, so I used the decreasing daylight to approximate the time.

Eileen came through the door when the light was completely gone from the one window in the room.

"Twenty minutes for dinner and lavatory break. Be back at your workspace by six twenty sharp. The doors will be locked at that time. Anyone not at their desk will lose their position, effective immediately."

I stood up and stretched the crick in my back from sitting for so long. My hands stunk from handling the tobacco, but the line to the washroom wrapped its way around the perimeter of the room. This was ridiculous. Locking people out if they were late? I thought that practice went out after the fatal Triangle Shirtwaist Factory fire eight years ago. Al and Ruth would be furious that this sort of thing was still going on.

I patted my bodice to make sure the little notebook and pencil were still hidden beneath my smock. I made my way to the back row where Florence was conversing with the girls seated next to her. She waved me off with a slight movement, which I took as a signal that she was discovering useful information. I walked past her, following a line of girls into the small room where I had hung my coat, and retrieved my dinner pail. I took a seat and unwrapped the cheese sandwich, bottle of milk, and apple that Mrs. Bumford made up for me in the dining hall back at school. Scanning the two rows of young women on either side of the table, I observed that most had less than my modest fare.

I kept a close eye on Mabel, who spoke to no one while she ate. When she gathered her things, replaced her dinner pail with the others stacked in piles, took her hat and coat down from the line of pegs on the wall, and left the room, I waited a few minutes before doing the same. I watched her put on her coat and leave the factory. I followed at a safe distance and hid in an alley when she entered the Brewster House. In a few minutes I heard a couple arguing as they departed the hotel, so I listened closely.

"I need more time. I'll get you the money as soon as I'm able."

"You agreed to pay back the loan the fifteenth of every month. You're late. I'm sorry, but it's coming out of your salary, unless we can come to a different arrangement."

"Please stop, Mr. Tussman. This isn't fair. I'm not

interested in any arrangement. My pa is bad off. I told you I'm good for the money, honest. Don't dock my pay. And stop being so familiar with me all the time. I mean it, get your hands off of me! Please, I'm begging you. I'm not that type of girl. Go back to Eileen. Let go of my arm! You're hurting me!"

"All the homely ones say they're not that type of girl. Get me my money and get it quick. And shut your mouth about Miss McKenna, or she'll be the one to fire you. Get back to work. Go on now, scoot!"

I crouched down to my knees, making myself as small as possible so as not to be seen. Reaching for my notebook and pencil, I copied the conversation between Larry Tassone and Mabel, word for word, while it was still fresh in my memory. After that, I wrote about the silence, the racially segregated work spaces, and the locked doors. Stuffing the notebook back down my bodice, I rushed back indoors to make it to my workspace in time.

Chapter Ten

"Harriet, the girl who sits next to me, told me the colored girls get paid half of what the white girls receive, and they're expected to open up in the morning before anyone gets here, bring in the tobacco leaves from the drying shed, stack them at each work station, and then begin work." Florence paused when the bus reached our stop in the village. Once we were walking on Main Street, she continued. "At the end of the work day, they sweep and mop both rooms as well as the staff room. I've logged and dated every incident of Larry Tassone's use of racial slurs toward us 'lazy, shiftless, good for nothing colored girls,' as well as ethnic insults toward the girls with foreign surnames. Basically, he hates everyone. And the things he says about his Cuban boss! I've got everything down to show Miss Wald."

"What a horrible person. I've got the unwanted advances he makes at everyone, stroking their cheek or touching their hair. But no one has it as bad as Mabel. He holds this so-called loan he made her over her head, threatens her with dismissal, and refuses to keep his hands off of her." I hid my notebook as we approached the entrance to the factory.

We were about an hour into work when Larry came into our room and approached Mabel's workspace. Wrenching her up out of her seat, he growled, "You, in my office, now."

I kept my eyes on my work as long as I could, until I heard someone cry out. I couldn't stand it any longer. I stood up.

"No, Jay, don't!" whispered Florence, but I ignored her.

I stormed out of the room toward the office to rescue Mabel, but Eileen got there first. I hid in the staff room, so I could listen to it all unfold.

"What in the— What the hell is going on in here?" she yelled, pulling Larry off Mabel.

Mabel ran past me, tore her coat from the peg, and left through the front door. Sobbing, she slammed it behind her.

"Baby, I can explain. The little tramp couldn't stay away from me. I lent her money, and she mistook my generosity for affection." Larry busied himself straightening his tie and smoothing his hair back into place.

"No, Lester." Eileen's voice broke. "I've heard this before. I tried to ignore the signs, but I'm not blind. I don't want to lose the little self-respect I have left. It's over. Fire me if you want, but it's over." Wow. For the first time in my life, I was proud of my sister.

I crept back to my workspace before Eileen came back into the stripping room.

"What happened?" whispered the young woman next to me.

"I don't know," I lied. "I lost my nerve and hid in the staff room."

After closing, I waited outside and told Florence I'd catch the next bus back to school. My nose was getting numb from the cold when Eileen finally came out.

176

"What are you still doing here?" she asked, wiping her eyes with a handkerchief. "Go home. It's late."

"Is there somewhere we can talk?" I asked, rubbing my gloved hands together to warm them.

"Why, so you can say 'I told you so'?" She walked ahead of me.

"There's something you should know," I said, running to catch up with her.

"That he's just another two-timing creep like the rest of them? Sorry, Jay, I'm not in the mood for another one of your lectures. Leave me alone."

"I know the perfect way you can get back at him," I yelled.

She stopped in front of the Southeast House and turned around.

"Do you want the whole village to know I've been dumped again?" she whispered. Opening the door to the hotel, she pushed me through. "Get in here. And for goodness sake, keep your voice down."

We were shown a table in the hotel restaurant, where I ordered tea and gingerbread. Eileen ordered scotch on the rocks.

"What do you mean, revenge?" she asked, lighting her cigarette.

"There's something you need to know. Florence and I are working undercover for the state government."

Eileen glugged her drink down, stood up, and slung her beaver coat across her shoulders. Throwing a handful of crumbled bills on the table, she proceeded toward the door.

I retrieved my pencil, wrote a number on her cocktail napkin, and ran after her. "Call Governor Smith if you don't believe me. I'm sure there's a phone in the hotel. Go ahead. Tell him you're my sister."

She grabbed the napkin and studied the number. Her eyes were swollen from crying, and her heavy pancake makeup was thinning out from falling tears, revealing her natural pale, freckled skin. In a voice raspy from too many cigarettes and gin, she glanced up at the Roman numerals on the huge clock in the vestibule and said, "You have five minutes."

Eileen ordered a second drink when the waiter brought my tea and slice of gingerbread topped with a dollop of whipped cream. Working against the black arrow minute hand ticking away on the clock, I started with my meeting with Miss Wald and Ruth, and explained everything about Tina, Mr. Hoyas's cooperation, and the real reason Pilar had been reading aloud in our stripping and booking room. I stopped at the five-minute mark and passed my notebook across the table to her. My gingerbread was still warm, so I dug into it while Eileen read my notes.

Minutes passed before she closed the book and passed it back to me. Her untouched, lit cigarette had burned down almost to the filter. She tapped it, the ashes descending into the glass ashtray imprinted with an image of the Southeast House.

"So you're a spy," she said. "I'll bet you and your little prep school chums have had a great laugh watching me throw myself at this creep." It was hard to believe this raspy, bitter voice was coming from my seventeen-year-old sister. Life had already hardened her.

She tapped my notebook with her fingertips. "I could have told you all of this if you just came to me, instead of sneaking around behind my back."

I took a deep breath and exhaled prior to responding so I could keep all emotion out of my voice, just as Tina had instructed me. "You would have told Larry what we were up to, and he would have left town, just as he's done over and over again for the past two years."

Eileen brought her hands to her face and rubbed her forehead with her fingertips. "Yes, you're right. And I'm no better than he is, actually. I knew what he was up to. I knew he was threatening and taking liberties with Mabel, but I was still mad at her because Artie cheated on me with her. I thought she deserved it. That's what jealousy does to someone. I stood by and watched him humiliate her. This is what I've become."

I took her hand away from her face and held it in mine, my first attempt at sisterly affection in years. "But you can help now, Eileen. You can bring this predator to justice. I've got all I can on this guy. What we need now is proof. A court can dismiss everything my friends and I have as circumstantial evidence. I need you."

She withdrew her hand and wiped her tears with a napkin. Composing herself, she nodded. "Okay. I'll help. He keeps all his books, the payroll, expenses, even his payoffs, locked in the top right-hand drawer of his desk. Every line he writes is doctored or downright fraudulent. He skims profits off the top and pockets them, shortchanges employees, everything you can think of. He's robbing the company blind. I'll steal the key tomorrow and distract him while you go in and grab them. Give them to your Miss Wald or Ruth. They'll know what to do."

I squeezed her hand. "Thank you."

She ignored my gesture. After taking a sip of scotch, she asked, "Any word from Jimmy Joe and that skank he's messed up with?"

"Nothing. Olive hasn't been in school since Nancy's parents confronted her at Smalley's. Jimmy Joe must have her hidden out of sight from Officer Belden somewhere." I missed Olive. I knew she was a troubled soul, but still, she had begun to open up to me before it all turned so bad at Smalley's.

"I think you and Packy are the only ones out of the lot of us who have their heads screwed on straight." Her laugh was dry and sad. "I've got to go home to tend the baby. I'll see you tomorrow afternoon." She dropped a crumpled dollar bill on the table and left.

Never in a million years would I have dreamed it would be my sister, Eileen, who would provide the evidence we needed to possibly bring this investigation to fruition. After asking the waiter for some change and the location of the pay telephone, I dialed Ruth's number and gave her the information Eileen shared with me. I told her I would have Larry Tassone's books for her investigators the following afternoon.

"Excellent! I'll contact Al and drive up tonight. Sheriff Stevens and some state troopers will be parked inconspicuously in the vicinity of the cigar factory for a stakeout. Plant someone near the front door to alert them when it's time. The troopers will take Tassone into custody, and my office will handle things from there. Well done, Jay."

"Don't congratulate me yet," I warned. "There's a million things that can go wrong before I can get those books into your hands."

If only I knew how prophetic my words would prove to be.

*

TUESDAY, DECEMBER 2, 1919
BREWSTER, NEW YORK

"I went to the telegraph office during lunch today," Pilar

180

said as we stopped briefly to collect ourselves on Main Street. "It was hard to let Papa know what we're about to do without making the telegraph operator suspicious."

"I felt the same way when I called Ruth from the hotel last night. I swear the operator was listening in. I thought I heard someone gasp when Ruth mentioned the state troopers would be parked somewhere along Main Street." I looked up and down the busy street. "Do you see any cars that may be them?"

"I hope your sister can keep Larry Tassone away long enough for you to unlock his desk and swipe his books," Florence said. "I didn't get much sleep last night worrying about what's about to happen."

"Tell me about it. My stomach has been turning somersaults since Eileen came up with this plan. Now you both have your logs to turn over to Ruth, right?"

Pilar patted her coat pocket. "I wrote down every word I heard the girls whispering while I was reading to them from *Jane Eyre*. Apparently most of them don't have the same affinity for Charlotte Bronte that I do. They call Larry 'The Octopus' because he's always got his hands on someone."

I opened the front door to the factory. "Here goes nothing."

I pulled the wretched center stems out of what felt like a thousand tobacco leaves before Eileen came over to inspect my work. "Shoddy workmanship, McKenna," she said.

After she moved on, I noticed the folded piece of paper beneath the leaf I was working on. I slowly covered it with my hand and lowered it to my lap. Turning left and right to make sure no one was watching me, I unfolded it with one hand. Within the note was a tarnished bronze key about two and a half inches in length. The handle was intricately designed with loops and curves. It felt heavy in my hand. I carefully slipped it in my smock pocket and read the note penned in Eileen's hand.

"Give me five minutes."

A cold sweat started to break out at the back of my neck. I reached back to touch the spot and found the tendrils of hair that escaped my hairpins were wet. My mouth felt like it was stuffed with cotton as I counted to sixty, five times, never stopping work. When I approximated five minutes, I tried to stand, but I couldn't make my right foot stop tapping the floor.

"Shush," whispered the girl next to me.

I put my hand over my forehead. "I feel faint. I need some air. Let me out."

The girl backed away, and I made my way to the hallway. Slipping past the closed door to the dining room, I heard Eileen and Larry arguing. I walked as quietly as possible down the hall until I came to Larry's office.

Clamping my mouth shut to stop my teeth from chattering, I entered and cautiously approached the oversized desk. A lit cigar was smoldering in an ashtray atop a pile of bills. A half-empty bottle of brandy and a snifter were staining unopened envelopes scattered across a green felt desk blotter. I felt for the key hole with my fingers on the right side of the desk. My hand shook uncontrollably as I fished for the key in my pocket. Willing the shaking to stop, I jiggled the key first right, then left until I felt a lock open. I silently pulled the drawer out along its groove until I saw the stack of black leather-bound books. I grabbed them and closed the drawer, pausing to lock it. Suddenly, I stopped. Someone was coming.

"How many times must I apologize, Eileen? I can't help

these girls throwing themselves at me. You of all people should understand what it's like to yield to temptation. Don't go masquerading as a woman of virtue at this stage of the game."

Larry opened the door to his office.

"Hey! What the hell are you doing in there! Give those to me now!"

I stood frozen to my spot, staring at Larry Tassone. He started toward me.

"Not so fast, Daddy."

Turning toward the sound of the calm voice, I watched in horror as Olive emerged from behind a bookcase near the hearth. Her long hair was cut short like a man's. I recognized the gun she was pointing at Larry's head as Jimmy Joe's military issue Colt .45 revolver.

"I'll get the police." Eileen turned to the door.

"No," I said. "Not yet." A strange calmness washed over me. "Let her explain."

"Put the gun down, Celeste," Larry said, taking a step toward Olive.

Olive pointed the gun at his forehead.

"How did— How did you get out?" he asked, swallowing hard.

"You never did give me enough credit. I bribed a guard at the Bedford Women's Reformatory and escaped. I was bound and determined to come for you, and I didn't care if I died trying. But I didn't die. And now you're going to." She pressed the gun against his right temple. "How does it feel, Daddy? How does it feel to be helpless and afraid?"

"Celeste, I never meant to hurt you, sweetie," he cooed, sweat gathering above his thin mustache. "Your mother was making all sorts of wild accusations. I had to send her away for her own—"

"She's dead. She died in that sanatorium where you had her locked away when she discovered the truth about what you were doing to me." She briefly waved the gun at me. "And now you're continuing to subject innocent girls in this factory to the same filthy behavior." She pulled back the hammer and cocked the gun, which made a clicking sound. A wet stain spread down the front of Larry's trousers.

"Olive," I said, keeping my voice low and steady, "the factory is surrounded by state troopers ready to take your father in. I've got all the evidence in these books, as well as a log of all of his inappropriate behavior with the employees. Pilar and Florence have written evidence as well. He'll be arrested and tried in court. If you leave now, he won't mention that this ever happened. Isn't that correct, Mr. Tassone?"

"I won't say a word," he sobbed. "Just don't kill me. Put down the gun, Celeste. I'm begging you!"

"You can sneak out the back way and hide until I can get you out of the village. Jimmy Joe will help me. Go now, before the troopers come in."

The instant Olive looked over to me for assurance, Larry wrenched the gun out of her hands. She kicked him hard, sending him to the ground, wailing in pain.

"Run!" I screamed.

Olive flew out of the room and I followed her, shouting at the top of my lungs. Larry grabbed my ankle as I neared the door.

"Give me those books or I'll shoot you dead right here," he growled as he pointed the gun up at me.

I tripped and dropped the books. I watched open-mouthed as they slid across the floor. I heard a loud bang and thought he shot me, but the sound was the door being kicked in.

Four enormous troopers in full uniform barged into the office and pointed their revolvers at Larry's head. He dropped the gun and struggled to get to his feet. As he was handcuffed, I scooped up the books.

"Jay, are you all right?" Ruth's worried expression turned to horror when she saw Jimmy Joe's revolver on the floor.

A trooper carefully picked it up with his gloved hand to avoid contaminating the gun with his fingerprints.

I got to my feet and handed Ruth the books before collapsing into her arms. "He was going to kill me for these," I cried, every muscle in my body trembling with shock and fear.

The trooper who picked up the revolver ushered Ruth and me out of the office. "I'm sorry, ma'am, but this is an active crime scene. You can't be in here."

Ruth turned around and poked the trooper in his chest. "I ordered this investigation and arranged for you and your fellow troopers to stake out the factory. Show a little respect, will you, son?"

"Excuse me, ma'am." The trooper blushed and tipped his hat at us.

"You shouldn't do that, Ruth. They're armed."

Ruth put her arm around my shoulder as she led me to the crowd waiting outside. "You nearly got yourself killed stealing the manager's books, but am I going to scold you about it?" She laughed. "The ends justified the means."

Miss Addison from the *Brewster Standard* rushed toward me with her pad and pencil. "Were you successful in getting Mr. Tassone's payroll and account books, Jay, as you planned?"

I knew that telephone operator was listening to my phone conversation the previous night.

Ruth brushed Miss Addison aside. "Miss McKenna has no comment, so please let us by."

"Jay!" Florence, Pilar, and Eileen ran straight at me, almost knocking me over.

Eileen grabbed me and hugged me tightly. "I thought you were dead! Why didn't you want me to get the police? That crazy girl had a gun, for Christ's sake!"

"I...I wanted to give Olive enough time to get away before the police could arrest her," I explained, still trying to catch my breath after all that had gone down this afternoon.

"Olive had a gun?" asked Florence. "What was she doing in Larry Tassone's office?"

"Apparently Larry Tassone is Olive's father, although he kept calling her Celeste for some reason," I tried to explain. "She was saying something about her mother dying in a sanatorium, and she mentioned escaping from the Bedford Women's Reformatory." I couldn't begin to process the words that were coming out of my own mouth.

"She escaped from a jail?" asked Pilar. "What was she in for, and how in the world did she ever get accepted at Haviland?"

"Absolutely no idea." I shrugged.

"Girls," called Ruth as she approached us with one of the troopers. "I'm afraid you're going to have to give your statements now while everything is still fresh in your heads."

"Of course," said Florence. She reached into her coat pocket. "Here's my logbook, Miss Lefkowitz."

"And mine," added Pilar.

"After we're finished with your statements, dinner's on me, girls. I can't begin to express how grateful Lillian, Al, and I are to you for nailing this creep. Your pay will be mailed to you, but I want to celebrate now. Let's go to Danbury, though. I know of a good restaurant on Main Street, and if we're lucky, news of Larry Tassone's arrest won't reach there for hours. What do you say?"

Eileen backed away. "I...I have to get back to work. If I still have a job, that is."

"Young lady, you've played a crucial role in this investigation, in spite of your not coming forward sooner." Ruth approached my sister and took her arm, leading her back to us. "The factory is currently a crime scene, so it is closed for the day. Please join us for dinner. I'll get you home in time to tuck your daughter in bed."

"Papa won't be happy that his factory is closed," said Pilar. "I assured him it wouldn't affect business."

"I'll telegraph Mr. Hoyas the minute we get to Danbury and assure him the crook has been caught and that he'll be back in business by morning." She pointed to Eileen. "And I'll recommend that Miss McKenna start as manager, provided she pledges to abide by my office's rules and regulations."

"I promise, Mrs. Lefkowitz," said a humbled Eileen.

"Hire Mabel Pugsley to fill your current position," I said.

"And pay every worker the same amount for the same job," added Florence.

Eileen put her hands up. "Okay, okay! Things are going to change. You have my word."

A honking horn coming up behind us made me jump. Henry leaned out the driver's side window of his father's feed truck. "I just heard and came as fast as I could. He jumped down from the truck and scooped me up off the ground in an embrace. After a long kiss, I glanced toward Ruth."

"Oh, all right. Bring him along too. Oy vey!" she cried.

Chapter Eleven

"You met *the* Lillian Wald?" Nancy clapped her hands in excitement. "Tell me all about her, and don't leave anything out."

It felt good to relax on the sofa with a cup of tea after such a harrowing few weeks. Having Nancy in the house made it so much more enjoyable to come home. We liked the same things, had the same points of view, and always seemed to find ourselves on Mam's bad side.

Mam called to us from the kitchen, "You two are suffering from the exuberance of your own pomposity. You think yourselves so grand with all your socialist ideas." She paused to take the screaming kettle off the gas. "That kind of thinking got us into war, I'll have you know."

"When I figure out what all that means, Mam, I'll try and have a better retort for you," I said, rolling my eyes at Nancy.

"I saw that, Josephine," said Mam as she came around the sofa with a tray bearing sliced brown bread, a crock of butter, and three steaming mugs of tea.

"Sorry, Mam," I murmured.

Quite out of character, Mam took a seat beside Nancy and me on the sofa. Looking down at her hands, scarred with burns and callouses, she spoke softly. "I suppose you two don't think I'm capable of using big words."

"That's not true, Mother McKenna," said Nancy. She attempted to take Mam's hands in hers, but my mother, in true McKenna fashion, recoiled from any physical contact with another human being.

"Call me Nonie, please. Mother McKenna sounds like a nun's name."

"Okay, Nonie." Nancy smiled as she tried out the name on her tongue.

"I know the two of you think I'm hopelessly old-fashioned," Mam said after she poured a bit of milk in her tea and slathered a slice of bread with butter. "Half of the time I've no idea what yer talking about with your newfangled ideas." Her voice trailed off as she took a bite of bread before reaching for her basket of yarn and knitting needles. Heaven forbid her hands remain idle.

"We don't think that way at all," said Nancy, wisely keeping her hands to herself this time.

"Of course you do. Thick as thieves, the two of you." Mam gave the skein of yarn to me to hold as she picked up the last stitch she had knitted of a sweater for baby Christine. "I'll have you know I had ideas and dreams once, when I first came to this country. My sister Bridie and I were planning on becoming modern American girls, what with our room in a boarding house and proper jobs in a trouser factory. Until we got laid off, we were enjoying dances at the Sons of Sligo society every Saturday night. I was quite a looker, if you could believe that." She chuckled, exposing a missing canine tooth.

"I've no doubt you were, as you still are," said Nancy. Jeez Louise, I hoped I wouldn't have to suck up to Henry's mom someday if we ever married.

"Go on with you." Mam cackled as she waved Nancy off, dropping a stitch.

"What happened, Mam?" I asked, boldly. We'd never had a frank conversation up to this point in my life. "Why didn't you just find another job after the factory let you go? Aunt Bridie must have, because she's still working as a telephone operator living in that nice apartment of hers in Washington Heights."

Mam turned her pinched face to mine. Seeing her pensive like this, not barking orders, made me aware of how fragile, of how painfully thin, she had become since Da's death last March.

She exhaled before responding. "Bridie was free to do as she chose. I was not."

"What do you mean, free?" I asked, dunking my brown bread in my tea to soften it. Sullivan snatched it from me and gobbled it up before I got a chance to take a bite.

Mam lowered her face to her knitting, her cheeks reddening a bit. "I found myself in the family way shortly after the landlord came banging on our door for the rent. Yer da offered to make an honest woman of me. He had a job with the railroad and a roof over his head. I had no choice but to accept."

"Holy moly." I hadn't seen that coming. "You mean you had to have a shotgun wedding because Jimmy Joe was on the way?" I asked, subtracting his age from their wedding date. It didn't add up. Maybe they lied about the year they were married.

Mam shook her head. "I miscarried the baby when I was about six months gone. I'd grown tired of your da's ranting by that point. Bridie begged me to have the marriage annulled and move into her new flat. She'd secured a good job with the telegraph office and said she could get me one as well. I didn't have the money for an annulment, and to tell you the truth, I was afraid of what yer da would do if I ran off on him."

I nodded, recalling Da's mood always simmering on the brink of boiling over. "Is that why Aunt Bridie and Da hated each other?" I asked, putting down the yarn so I could toss a new log on the fire. I stoked it, a spray of coral and blue cinders shooting up in the hearth.

Mam nodded. "Aunt Bridie felt Da robbed me of my freedom, and Da resented her for putting ideas in my head and having airs about her. Bridie can come and go as she pleases, and me, well I'm stuck here on this godforsaken farm with yet another baby to raise."

"Why don't you get off this godforsaken farm once in a while then?" I asked. "The whole town showed up for the veteran's parade last month. All of your friends were asking for you."

"And you used to love going to your altar and rosary meeting at the church," added Nancy. "And what happened to Catholic Daughters? Why did you stop going after Christine was born? You've got to get out more."

"And listen to all the tongues wagging about Eileen's bastard daughter?" Mam said. "No thank you." She stuck her knitting needles in the skein in my hand.

"Well then, you've got no one to blame but yourself if you're lonely," I said, waiting for a slap that did not come.

"Come with Jay and I for lunch at the Southeast House tomorrow," Nancy offered. "My treat."

"Yes, come, Mam," I chimed in. "The gingerbread is to die for."

"Ah, you two communists are feeling guilty now that I've shared my tale of woe." Mam laughed as she stood up, her knee joints cracking with arthritis. "Just don't write me off as a bitter old woman. As I said, I had dreams once. I'm off to bed."

"She hasn't had an easy life," Nancy commented once Mam shut the bathroom door behind her.

"No, she hasn't." I pulled a crocheted throw blanket around my shoulders and settled in before the fire blazing in the hearth. Sullivan snored in my lap, so I was careful not to spill any of my still-hot tea on him. I had forgotten how soft the fur on his ears was, or how adorable his snoring sounded when he changed positions while he slept.

I was starting to doze off when I heard the crunch of Henry's father's truck coming up the packed dirt driveway. Sullivan tore his way out of the crocheted throw and leapt across the coffee table, toppling the tea tray, before flying into the kitchen to bark, jump, and scratch at the back door.

"Stop the racket," yelled Mam as she emerged from the bathroom in her wrapper to let Henry in from the cold.

"Thought you might be up for a movie. *Daddy Long Legs* with Mary Pickford is playing at the Cameo," he said, although the way he widened his eyes at me when Mam turned away let me know we were not going to a movie. "Nancy, why don't you and Packy come along, my treat. Eileen too, if she's around."

Nancy caught the look in Henry's eyes as well. "Eileen took the baby to see Santa Claus at Luckey Platt in Danbury. Packy's working on the books, but if you give me a minute, I'll ask."

Mam stared Henry up and down as if he committed a major breach of etiquette. "My son may be a cripple,

Henry, but I'll have you know he can certainly afford to pay for his own movie ticket."

"I didn't mean any offense, Mrs. McKenna. I was just being neighborly is all," he stuttered, shooting me another more urgent look.

"So what's this all about?" asked Packy as the four of us squeezed into the front seat of the truck. Nancy had to sit on Packy's lap for all of us to fit, but he didn't seem to mind at all.

"Jimmy Joe stopped by the feed store today and told me to bring all of you to meet him at that bar he hangs out at in the village. Said it was important."

"Maybe it's something about Olive. I told her to hide out until I could find Jimmy Joe, but it was a madhouse that day, and the next thing I knew we were in Danbury having dinner with Ruth. Hope she found him okay." I felt guilty all of a sudden.

"Celeste, I mean Olive, can take care of herself," Nancy assured me.

"How do you know her name is Celeste?" I asked, confused. Nancy wasn't there in Larry's office that day.

"You never were a good liar," Packy drawled.

"Will someone please explain to me what's going on?" I asked.

"We're here," Henry said as he parked the truck in front of the bar. "I'm sure Jimmy Joe will explain everything."

The bar was dark and smelled of stale beer and ammonia. My boots stuck to the floor, and the air was thick with cigar smoke. Several old men crouched protectively over their drinks at the bar, spittoons at their feet. Jimmy Joe's cronies from the war, one with his pant leg pinned up where his leg used to be, played cards at battered tables. The chairs they sat on looked as if they were hurled across the bar more than once.

Jimmy Joe threw down his hand, collected his money from the table, and swigged down whatever beer was left in his mug.

"This way." He motioned us to a flight of stairs with threadbare remnants of carpeting on each step.

"Nice to see you too," I murmured as I made my way up the creaking stairway. The handrail was worn smooth from decades of work-calloused hands. Da had told me immigrants who'd worked on the reservoirs and the railroad used to board in this building. I supposed if I could escape getting shot to death this week, I could survive whatever was waiting at the top of those stairs.

The top landing led to an even darker hallway that smelled of mold, burnt toast, and urine, and I wasn't talking cats.

Packy stumbled a bit because the floor sloped downward. "Only the finest accommodations for the lady, I see," he said after he righted himself.

"Shut up," said Jimmy Joe as he fit his key in the lock at one of the two doors off the hallway. "This is the only place I can hide her without someone ratting her out to Sheriff Stevens. I know I can trust my friends at the bar."

Through the cigarette haze in the single room, bare except for a dresser, a kerosene lamp and a saggy bed, I made out Olive shoving a few things in that godforsaken bag of hers. The walls were covered in peeling, faded paper that in the previous century boasted a floral print. Now its only purpose was to hide the black mold growing beneath the once pretty patterns.

"Jay." She smiled for a minute before we all crowded into the miniscule room. "What's all this about?" she asked suspiciously.

"Be nice. They've come to say goodbye," said Jimmy Joe.

"We have?" I asked.

"Sit down," said Jimmy Joe.

I looked around the tiny room. "Where?"

"I'll go grab a couple of chairs from downstairs. Give me a hand, Henry."

Henry kicked on the door a few minutes later after humping six chairs up the stairs. Jimmy Joe joined us a while later, balancing two pitchers of beer in one hand and six glasses in the other.

"So what's up?" I asked as Henry handed me a dirty glass of beer. I wiped the rim of the glass on my sleeve before taking a tentative sip of the warm, bitter brew.

"I don't think it's fair to keep Jay in the dark any longer," said Nancy, placing her untouched glass of beer on the floor next to mine.

"You're right," said Packy, placing his hand on her knee. "Jimmy Joe met me when I was making my milk deliveries the Monday after Nancy's parents confronted Celeste at Smalley's. He and Celeste were staying at a cold water shack with the German bakers from Dieter's right outside the village. Nancy and I met them there."

"I brought some of my clothes for Celeste," said Nancy, "but Jimmy Joe thought it would be better if she was disguised as a man until he could get her out of town since the police were looking for her. I had come straight from work, so I had my gauze-cutting shears in my bag. I cut Celeste's hair for her so it would be easier to be taken for a man. She dressed in Jimmy Joe's clothes to complete the disguise."

"Okay, so? What next?" I asked. "Are you going to parade around as a man for the rest of your life to avoid being recognized by the cops? And why is everyone calling you by a different name now? You know Larry Tassone, or rather your father, will sing like a bird in court even though he promised not to mention your trying to shoot him."

"Of course he will," Olive said, stubbing out her cigarette and draining her glass.

Nancy continued. "I confronted Celeste about her morphine addiction—"

"I can tell it," Olive interrupted. "Jay, my name's not Olive Moody. I'm Celeste Tassone."

"I'm so confused," I said. "How did you get into Haviland after escaping from jail and robbing Nancy's parents?" I turned to Nancy. "And why are you of all people helping her to avoid the police? Your poor father looked about ready to have a stroke when he recognized her in the bar."

"You heard me confront my father about the disgusting things he did to me, and how he had my mother sent to an insane asylum when she tried to press charges. When I was left alone with him, I ran away to try and get my mother out of the sanatorium. When I ran out of money, a cop found me living on the streets in the Bronx, where I'm from, and brought me home. My father told the police officer I was a truant, a thief, a habitual liar, and that he couldn't care for me any longer. I was sent to a juvenile detention center. I was constantly trying to escape so I could get to my mother, so my stay there kept getting extended until I aged out and was sent to the Bedford Reformatory. It was there that I met Olive Moody. Olive came from a rich family, but she was wild. She didn't want to live the life her mother had carved out for her."

She paused here and sipped from the beer glass Jimmy Joe refilled for her. "Thank you, love." She patted his hand and continued. "Olive was bad to the bone like me, so of course, we bonded instantly. She was serving a short sentence for public drunkenness, theft, and resisting arrest. We got into all sorts of trouble together, and loved every minute of it. And then she introduced me to morphine."

She rested her head on Jimmy Joe's shoulder for a minute before continuing with her story. He wrapped his long arm around her shoulders.

"At first it was fun. Just another stunt we pulled to get us through the miserably hard days and long nights in prison. Olive's boyfriend slipped it to her when he'd come to visit. Then I grew dependent on it. Olive was coming up for parole. She was only fifteen, so her mother enrolled her in Haviland in an attempt to rehabilitate her when she got out. Olive had no intention of going. Mrs. Moody brought her everything she needed for school, the uniform, the coat, even the ridiculous napkin ring and teaspoon. She was planning to escort Olive straight from the reformatory to Haviland on the day of her release. She was taking no chances."

Celeste took a long swig of beer before continuing. "Then Olive got sick. Tuberculosis, the doctor in the infirmary told her. I guess the morphine had masked the pain in her lungs until she was too far gone. She died on September tenth, my eighteenth birthday." She stopped and stared at her hands for a few minutes. "I never felt so alone in my whole life. I needed to be with my mother, and I was hurting bad from morphine withdrawal at this point. I had no money to buy it from the wardens. They could get you whatever you wanted, but you needed cash. I knew I had to get out of there and make some money, somehow."

"But how?" I asked, leaning forward in my rickety chair. "You were in prison. There must have been guards at every turn." I looked at Celeste with new eyes. I could never have survived half of what she had described so far.

"I came up with a plan. No one ever came for Olive's school uniform. On visiting day, I sweet-talked a guard into letting me outside to get a little air. Once outdoors, I picked a lock and made my way into the secure area where inmates' personal belongings are kept until their release. I found Olive's Haviland uniform along with her registration papers and some cash. I changed into her clothes in a staff locker room and made my way to the visitors' room. The guards there mistook me for someone visiting an inmate, so I just walked out with a family when they were leaving."

"Just like that?" I asked, astounded. "Didn't anyone in the family ask who you were?"

Celeste shook her head. "The parents were too busy blaming each other for what had driven their daughter into 'a life of debauchery,' as the father put it. Funny, I can still hear the father spitting out that word as if it were yesterday." She stubbed her cigarette out in a chipped saucer. "Once outside, I lived on the cash in Olive's purse. I bought morphine from a dealer and made my way to the sanatorium in Katonah, where I found out my mother had died from the Spanish flu. I was crushed and considered killing myself so I could be with her in heaven. And then I grew more and more enraged when I realized who was responsible for my mother's death and my desire to end my life at eighteen years of age. I decided to hunt my father down and make him pay for what he did to us."

"With no money, no one to turn to for help, and literally nothing except the clothes on your back. How did you manage to find him?" Celeste's story was beginning to sound like something out of a Dickens novel.

"I gave his name to every factory in the area until some-one tipped me off that he had taken a job in Brewster. Over the summer I decided to take a gamble and enroll at Haviland under Olive's name. I figured I had nothing to lose, and it would bring me closer to my target. I made my way to Carmel. Once I reached Croton Falls, I was hurting bad with morphine withdrawal. I was sweating profusely, burning up with fever, and throwing up any food I man-aged to get my hands on. I spent days crouched up in a ball, seized with stomach pains. I needed more morphine money." She turned to Nancy. "That's when I asked your parents if I could spend the night. I took off with cash, war bonds, and anything that I thought I could pawn. I'm sorry. They were such nice people. I was desperate to stop the pain, and only morphine could do that."

"It's an unforgiving drug," said Nancy. "So what did you do with the money, after you bought more morphine?"

"Call it dumb luck or divine intervention, but the ad-missions office at Haviland bought my story, accepted cash for my fall tuition payment, and here I am. At least I found Jimmy Joe, or rather, you brought me to him, Jay."

I stayed quiet for a while, stunned at her story. "Olive's mother never found you out?" I asked.

Celeste shook her head. "I'm sure she would have, even-tually. Why do you think I pledged that ridiculous guild? When Nathalia told me Olive's mother was an alumnus, I knew I had no choice. Mrs. Moody is sure to get a bill for the spring semester, but I'm not sticking around to find out."

Now I understood why the pledging I found so grueling was nothing to Celeste. She had survived abuse and prison. Scrubbing toilets must have been a piece of cake to her.

"So when you went out at night, you were buying drugs?" I asked.

"No. I had dealers in Carmel and Brewster for that. Both are doctors, if you can believe that." She smiled sadly. "At night I used. That's why you found me asleep in the outhouse. I couldn't sleep at night after Olive and my mother died without a lot of morphine. Mainly though, I was out looking for my father. When I spotted him that Saturday in Smalley's, I knew I was going to kill him. He looked so smug and condescending with your sister. When I finally tracked him down to the cigar factory, I stole Jimmy Joe's gun. You know the rest."

"So now what?" I asked.

"We're leaving for Florida first thing in the morning," said Jimmy Joe. "Key West, to be exact. A buddy of mine from the marines, coincidently named Buddy, wrote me before Nancy's parents identified Celeste in Smalley's. He was looking for a partner on his fishing boat. I wasn't sure about making such a big move, but now it seems like the perfect solution. I can get Celeste far enough away to get the police off her back, and I can start anew. There's too many ghosts up here for me."

He stood up and put his hand on Packy's shoulder. "You know the business end of the farm far better than I do, and Felix and Ernie are happy to get the work. You can afford to bring them on full time now. And once Prohibition starts, you'll be making money hand over fist selling applejack and moonshine." He grinned at Henry. "There'll be plenty of cash available for a young man who can learn how to install a still in our barn, as well as on every other farm in this county."

"Tell him about the stop you'll be making along the way, Jimmy Joe," said Nancy.

"Oh, right. Nancy did some research and found an excellent drug rehabilitation facility for women in Georgia.

They've a great success rate with women addicted to morphine sulfate. Celeste has agreed to spend some time there until she can get off that poison."

"As long as you'll come for me when I'm well again," Celeste added, looking up at Jimmy Joe.

"Of course. None of this adventure means anything without you," he said, taking her hand in his. "I want to spend the rest of our lives taking all the pain away, naturally."

Wow, they really loved each other.

"But, Nancy," I said, confused. "I still don't get why you've gone to all this trouble for someone who robbed your parents."

"Celeste is good for Jimmy Joe. She calms him, soothes him, and has given him a purpose in life. She's more broken than he is. He wants to rescue her," Nancy said. "And I believe referring her to the drug rehabilitation facility in Georgia is something that Lillian Wald would have done."

I couldn't argue with that.

"I'm wiring you the money Celeste stole from your parents once I start earning a steady salary on the boat," said Jimmy Joe. "Buddy tells me the waters off the Keys are filled with dolphinfish, marlin, and grouper, and rich folks can't get enough of them on restaurant menus. I'm dying to reel one in."

I emptied the contents of my purse and handed it to Celeste. "Here, take this. I can't bear to think of you traveling with nothing but that ratty old bag. Throw it in the stove downstairs and burn it."

Celeste shook her head and held tightly to her bag. "Never. This was my mother's grocery bag. It's all I have left of her."

Chapter Twelve

The world was silent this morning, save for the stout cardinals, perched like cherries on the snow-covered branches of the sweeping evergreens. The crisp, cloudless sky was crystalline blue, the air clean and sharp. Haviland's campus was spread thick with a layer of meringue snow whipped by the wind into stiff peaks. I brought my mittened hands up to warm my cheeks, made ruddy by the cold. After trudging through half a foot of snow from Fowler House to my cherished spot in the woods by the creek that Florence and I discovered, I felt for the precious envelope in my coat pocket. It was in there, safe and ready for reading.

Fortunately, after almost losing her friendship over the whole Gilded Lily disaster, Florence and I had shared all our special occasions here ever since. After one of our talks under the shade of the pines, Florence convinced me to tell the truth about how I got my concussion to Miss Chichester, who took matters into her own capable hands. As a result, she wisely came to a compromise with the guilds. While she realized prohibiting a Haviland tradition of over fifty years old was unlikely, she mandated that all guilds be overseen by a faculty advisor to ensure safe, dignified, and appropriate pledging rituals. This action resulted in my exclusion from all guild-sponsored activities, such as this evening's Valentine's Day Dance. When I reflected upon last year's disaster at this event, it was with unadulterated joy that I embraced the guilds' collective decision.

Surprisingly, Evangeline, Helen, and even Nathalia did not share the guilds' opinion of me. While they didn't embrace me, they didn't give me a hard time for going to Miss Chichester. Of course, once Nathalia's mother got wind of Mae and Doris sending her home after she refused to swim Lake Gleneida, the Gilded Lilies decided to make an exception and accept Nathalia as the single new member of their esteemed sisterhood.

Sitting on this stone wall with my face turned up to the winter sun, I realized how deeply fulfilling it was to enjoy the true friendship of the girls in the attic. Huddled around the fire this winter among the sweater-garbed cats and squirrels, we shared our stories, our journeys to Haviland, and our dreams. We laughed about the quirkiness of our landladies and reveled in being the outsiders that we were. While I wouldn't turn down the furniture, plumbing, steam heat, and electricity of the dorm, I didn't miss the company.

And now it was time to open the treasured letter that was delivered in this morning's post. It was from Jimmy Joe.

January 20, 1920
Dear Jay,

*Hope this finds you freezing your hide off while we enjoy trop-
ical weather in the dead of winter. Just kidding. We have found
paradise, though, no doubt about that. The water's jumping
with tuna and swordfish, and nothing beats coming back with
a boat full of them to sell. I'm a regular pinhooker now. Buddy
says that's what you call fishermen who sell the catch of the day
to restaurants.*

*Buddy has been a stand-up guy since I arrived. I stayed with
him and his wife when I first got here. He showed me the ropes
on his boat and gave me my first rod and reel. Says I'm a natural
fisherman, for a farm boy, that is. I'm full partner in the business
now, and the money's coming in.*

*Took some time off earlier in the month to head up to Georgia
to get Celeste. She looks like a new woman since they cured her of
that poison. She's ready for a new life as a fisherman's wife, and
that's just what I made her after we made an appointment with
the first preacher we could find once we came back to Florida.
Mam's sure to have a cow once she finds out she was no Catholic,
but that never much mattered to me. All's I know is that there
are no atheists in the foxholes, and since I've been in one, one
preacher is as good as another.*

*Anyway, the bride and I have set up home in two rooms on
Duvall Street. You'd love it here, Jay. There's some real interest-
ing characters down here. Lots of boys who fought alongside me
as well. I belong here. I couldn't find my way up north, but now
I'm home. I've cut back on the booze, and I'm trying hard to make
my peace with what happened during the war. What I'm trying
to say is, I'm learning what it feels like to be content.*

*Give my regards to the family, and let me know how Packy
is getting along with the farm. There's nothing much going on
now, I'm sure, but things are bound to get busy come spring. Kiss
that ugly baby of Eileen's for me, and break the news of my marriage to Mam, will you? Since you're the only one who can write*

halfway decent, drop me a line and let me know how everybody's getting on.

In the enclosed envelope you'll find some money from my earnings. Please give Nancy most of it as my first installment of paying her back the money Celeste stole from her parents. Celeste wants you to have what's left over as payment from the cash she stole from your trunk in the attic. She'll be apologizing to you in her letter to you, which you should expect shortly.

Would sure love for you to come and visit sometime. It's real nice here, and I know you have a friend whose family is from this neck of the woods. Maybe you could travel with her. Take care, now.

Your brother,
James Joseph McKenna

Key West. I couldn't even imagine traveling to an exotic tropical island. But then again, maybe I could. Pilar would have to go home to visit once school let out. So far, this school year brought me more than my fair share of adventures. I had grown confident and strong. Why not plan for the trip of a lifetime?

What was real?

Researching a book for me is like a treasure hunt through archival newspapers. I first get a feel for minor events that lend authenticity to the story. In the case of *Beyond Haviland*, I noticed advertisements about popular car models of the day, articles on post-war sugar and coal shortages, and movies starring Mary Pickford and Lillian Gish, popular film stars of the day. This type of information provides a picture of the times for the reader.

While I'm fishing for information that will help form the backdrop of the story, I've got one eye out for news events that may provide a kernel of a story, something that will spark my imagination to build into a satisfying plot for the reader. In the case of *Beyond Haviland*, two articles caught my attention. One was about a record-high enrollment for the September 1919 semester at Drew Seminary for Girls in Carmel, New York, which is the inspiration for my fictional Haviland Seminary. The article mentioned that several students had to board at the home of the Misses Reed. This article brought the fictional Tillie and Hazel Fowler to life.

The second article that sparked my imagination was about one Edith Moody, an eighteen-year-old former prisoner of The Bedford Reformatory, who received shelter at the home of D. A. Outhouse in Jefferson Valley, New York. Mr. Outhouse reported that after Miss Moody left his home some time before daybreak, he noticed $500 worth of articles belonging to his family were missing. Wondering what would cause a girl to be sentenced to prison, then be paroled, only to rob a house led to the creation of Olive Moody.

I became introduced to Lillian Wald through her written correspondence as part of an archival collection of the New York Public Library. Lillian Wald founded the Henry Street Settlement in lower Manhattan and was a coveted speaker for agencies all over the state, the country, and the world. I don't know if she ever worked with Belle Moskowitz, political advisor for Governor Alfred Smith, who was the inspiration for the fictional Ruth Lefkowitz, but I thought the three of them, with Jay, Florence, and Pilar, would form a wonderful alliance in the fight for fair labor practice and safe conditions for workers.

I hope you enjoyed the second book in the Haviland Series. I'm about to begin research on the third book, which will set Jay off on an adventure in Key West, Florida. That research should be fun!

Acknowledgements

Well before I begin a new story, I begin scanning archival issues of the *Putnam County Courier* and the *Brewster Standard* newspapers for articles that will inspire character and plot development. Many thanks to the staffs of the Brewster, Carmel, and Mahopac public libraries for making these newspapers available online. During my visits to H.H. Wells Middle School, Mahopac High School, and North Salem Middle School to talk about my book research, I recall how, before the internet era, I used to have to lug out huge hardbound copies of these newspapers or thread microfiche film through a projector at the Brewster Library to conduct my research. Access to online archival newspapers makes research so much easier than it used to be.

I'd like to thank Sarah Johnson and the staff of the Putnam County Historian's office, and Amy Campanaro, Director of the Southeast Museum, for the use of their 1919-era postcard images on my webpage, deborahraffertyoswald.com, as well as for the cover of *Beyond Haviland*. These images lend a wonderful authenticity to the book. I'd also like to thank the Brewster History Exchange group for their priceless memories of the Prohibition era in Brewster, New York.

Special thanks to Lonna Kelly for her talent in designing a website with images that highlight the local history behind the books. Thank you to my amazing beta readers, Lynn Lamont, Michelle Messemer, Phyllis Rieder, and Virginia Tait, for the time and effort you put forth in reading and revising the first draft of the story.

Lastly, thank you to the two amazing Lisas. Lisa Fields, a talented artist, created the beautiful cover based on vintage postcards and a 1919 fashion catalogue page to bring Jay, Florence, and Pilar to life. Lisa Gilliam, an amazing editor, brought the story from manuscript to formatted book. I'm so very grateful for your professionalism and expertise.

35405098R00130